In This Sleep of Death

A novel

Margo Haas

In This Sleep of Death
by
Margo Haas

Copyright © 2018 by Margo Haas
Published in the United States by Grover Hill Press.

All rights reserved. No part of this book may be used or reproduced in any manner, including internet usage, without written permission of the author.

This is a work of fiction. Names, characters, places, and incidents are either the product of the author's imagination or are used fictitiously. Resemblance to actual persons, living or dead, events or locales is entirely coincidental.

Edited by Carlo DeCarlo

Plays by Margo Haas

The Missing Choir of Soda Springs
Chilly Dog and Other Plays
Lost in the Bermuda Triangle
Christmas at the Wiley Diner
Texaco Star
Sacred Hearts

For Casper and Thea

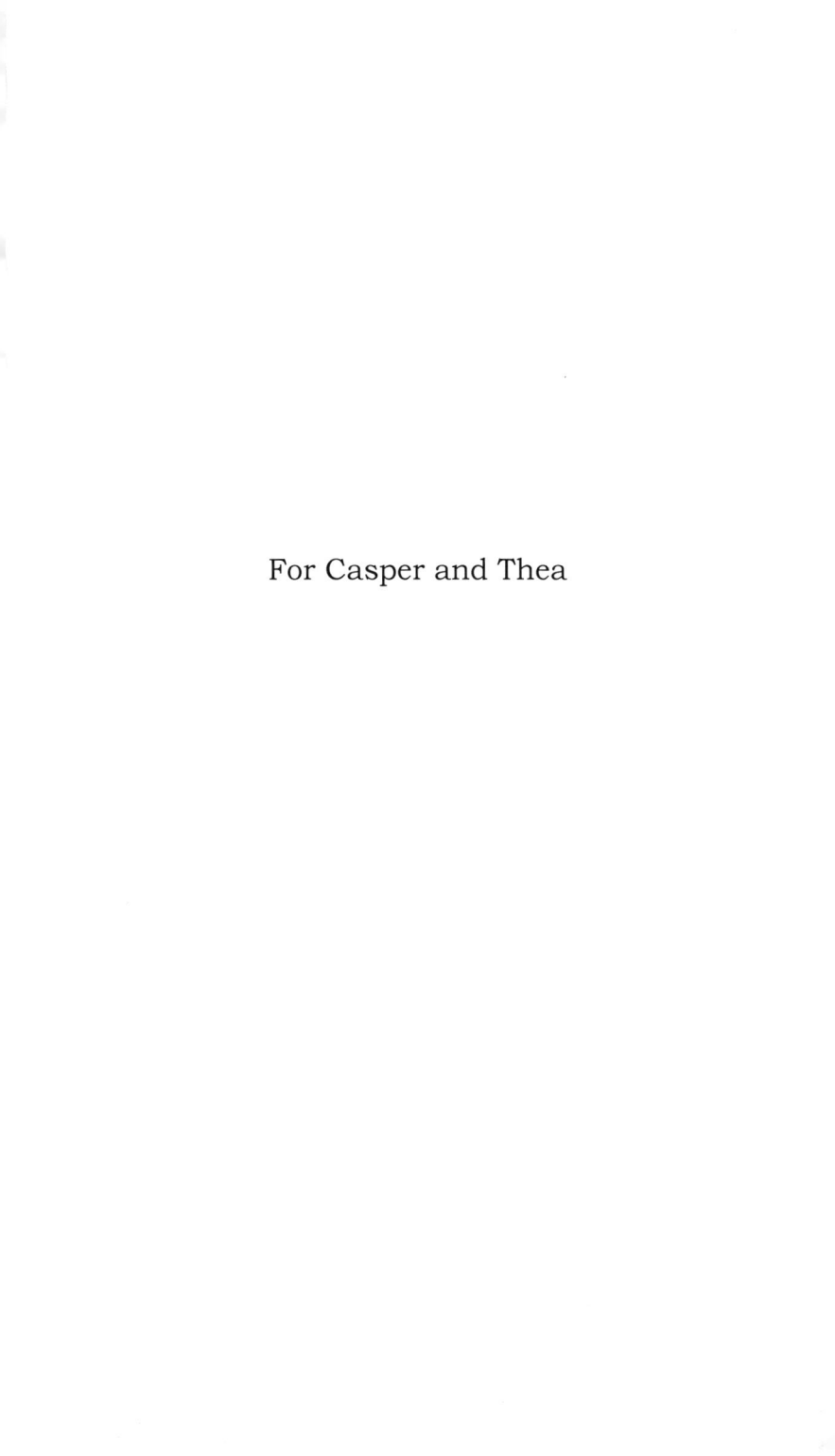

THE INCIDENT

After I killed him, I placed the body deep enough into the ground for it to go undetected. At least I think I did. Sometimes, though, in the black of night, I wonder if a raccoon or wandering coyote smelled the damp flesh or residual blood beneath the surface and dug him up. Not that either of those creatures could drag a human being up and out of a deep hole. But they could, possibly, do just enough damage to expose my secret, leaving the grave disrupted and the corpse right there in plain view for any weekend hiker or forest ranger to see.

I would go back and check the grave myself if I could remember where it was. I've tried, but my thoughts always come up empty. In fact, I don't even know if it was a man I killed. I think it was a man. In a white shirt. I've been wondering lately how I did it. Or, for that matter, why I did it and how I buried him. These are the pressing questions that keep a girl up at night. Occasionally the thoughts creep into my head in study hall, but there are enough distractions in there to take my mind off murder for a while. It's in the quiet of my dreams at night that the fears come roaring back.

Details of the crime are fuzzy and just out of reach, like a thick cloud blocking the sun. You would think the memory of something that bad would be right there in my face, screaming at me, shaking its fist in disgust and yelling *murderer, murderer!*, but it hasn't (yet) and so no judgment has been passed down. It's only a matter of time, though. I know this because in the last several months my dreams have begun to tell my story.

I see the gritty earth before me, dirt flying, a limb dragging. A shoe rolling down a hill. I can almost make out the shoe. A Nike, I think. I wake up shaking and try to recall more, but nothing emerges. This isn't a dream-dream, the kind with crazy story lines and no endings. This is the same dream, the very same.

I've never told anyone about this, of course, because confessing to a murder means the end of life as I know it. Not that my life's that great, but it's better than jail, which is where I would be headed. You know—the slammer, the big house, up the river. And it wouldn't matter that I'm fifteen years old. Courts today have prosecuted killers as young as eleven years old. Imagine, eleven years old, just three years older than my little brother, Tyler.

What, though, would I be confessing to anyway? I have no details, yet I know they're there, sitting on the sidelines just waiting for the take.

If I were to tell my parents about this, they would laugh—and not in a good way. They don't get me. I'm just someone who puzzles them, someone who freaks out at the noise of jet engines and the idea of Halloween haunted houses.

When I was in middle school and mixing with kids who were having a good time, I would be there, but fretting on the inside. I worried that the earth would suddenly stumble on its axis and interrupt gravity, throwing the world into unspeakable chaos. I worried that my cat, Sheba, was going blind because my brother sprayed her with Windex in a stupid attempt to remove her fleas. I worried that my father would die in a car crash on his way home from a road trip.

I try not to be so serious. My mother says it's putting lines on my face. Oh, what a horrible thought!

Outside of my parents and maybe my older cousin Tia—who's always telling me to lighten up—people do, thankfully, see me as a regular person, an average sophomore at Glenview High in the average town of Barton in the average state of Ohio. In fact, our township and everybody in it is so average I don't think they would know interesting if it was right in front of them. Our city's most recent accomplishment was its scale model of the White House made entirely from recycled bleach bottles. It's downright embarrassing.

But this all works in my favor because I can blend without being noticed. I go to the occasional party or movie just enough to not be branded a total introvert like Calista Meyer, who, according to reliable sources, has only spoken aloud once in class, and that was to say no, she was not trying out for drama club after her name appeared on the sign-up sheet outside the gym.

But the truth is, I wouldn't mind being like Calista. She's about as invisible as a person can be and still pass for human. She can float through the halls like a specter, knowing no one is going to ask her what she did over the weekend or whether she thought John Sabatini was the hottest guy on the wrestling team. Maybe she worries all the time, too, and sees dismal flashes of an abhorrent deed long suppressed. Maybe she, too, knows she has no real allies in the world, for who would those people be?

Some may say that since I am so young and scared and possess no apparent motive, that I couldn't possibly have committed a murder. But I did. I am as sure of it as I am the sun will rise tomorrow. It happened, and, because I am basically a decent person, I chose to bury (a weird pun) the details along with the body. Some things are just too heinous to keep on the front burner.

Make no mistake, I would prefer to recall none of this, but the dreams keep coming, like a forging river after a violent storm, and I have no choice. It possesses me. It controls me from the inside and leaves me with no fight left on the outside. I can deny and pretend, but it doesn't matter. What I have to figure out is how to stop the dreams and how to block the thoughts. I have to figure out how to reconcile that, though I was driven to kill, I appear to the outside world, even to myself at times, to be a nice person. This doesn't make for lighthearted living.

My mother says she gave up on me years ago, that no child is as intense as I am. Maybe she's right. Maybe that's what drove me to murder.

CHAPTER ONE

Tyler isn't up yet, and if he thinks I'm going to go in and nag him out of bed, he's crazy. It's enough I'm fixing his breakfast, a task he's perfectly capable of executing himself. I mean, any little kid can pop a frozen waffle into a toaster then dump syrup on it, but my mother asked me to prepare it for him, that all-important first meal of the day. This really has very little to do with nutrition and a good start, though; it's about her perpetual guilt at rarely being home for her son. My father isn't around that much either, but it seems fathers often get a pass on ignoring the daily functions of their kids.

My mother has left yet another sticky note on the counter, this one reminding me to take a lasagna from the freezer and put it in the oven at four o'clock. My God, can't she do anything? I had planned to go to Fabric City where she works, after school. Not to see her—in fact, if our paths didn't cross that would be fine—but to buy more materials for my fabric collage. I also need to go to the library, and now, because of the stupid lasagna, I'll have to postpone it.

I'm actually glad that once Tyler is on the bus I'll be alone. The high school is less than a ten-minute walk from our house, which gives me almost forty-five minutes to do homework.

I used to come home from school and finish most of my assignments before dinner, leaving my evenings free. But since the dreams have become more intense, I find I can hardly stay awake during the day. Lately I come home and fall asleep on the sofa for a couple of hours. It's the best sleep I get. I rarely dream then.

My mother hates my naps. "You need to go to bed earlier, Helen. You're too young to be so tired all the time." She and my father see my night vigils as a character flaw. They have no idea I'd love to go to sleep earlier, as early as Tyler even, but when I sleep, I dream. And when I dream, it's bad.

"Helen?" Tyler is standing next to me now. His haphazard bed-head looks like a lunatic's, and I notice that he's wearing his pajama top backward. He's a helpless mess.

"Yeah?"

"I need money for a field trip."

"How much?"

"Ten dollars. We're going to the art museum in Kent."

"Call Mom and tell her to drop it off at school, Tyler. I don't have ten dollars."

"Yes, you do."

"No, I don't."

I do. But there are the waffles. And the lasagna. I have to draw the line somewhere. Let my mother handle it. My father escapes these crises since he travels so much for work.

"The trip is this morning." Tyler starts to whine. "I was supposed to have the money in last week." He looks much younger than eight standing there with his pajama top on wrong.

"Fine." I slam the milk carton down on the counter for effect.

"And can you sign my permission slip?"

Forging my mother's signature is the easy part; I've been doing it for years, not out of desperation but rather for convenience.

I pack Tyler's lunch while he eats two Eggo waffles. I'm eager to get him out of the house so I can finish the next chapter of our book for health class, *The 7 Habits of Highly Effective Teens*. I find this book only loosely related to health, but to hear our teacher talk it's a wonder anyone survived before it was in print.

So far, I find the book oddly unsettling. The first habit listed, "Be Proactive", which really means taking responsibility for one's choices. While reading that chapter I felt myself growing irritated, almost angry, so I just skimmed through the rest.

I'm secretly hoping that somehow this book can help me get a handle on my incessant worrying. For instance, I'm now slightly concerned that Tyler's teacher will recognize the forgery on his permission slip and call my mother. Of course, in this case I can throw the bad parent card at my mother and probably stop that one in its tracks. She feels so awful that she ignores Tyler, I have accumulated a fully stocked arsenal of guilt ammo ready to fire at the enemy.

My mother doesn't feel any guilt about me because, as she loves to tell anyone who will listen, she, Melanie Wren, stayed home with her daughter until she walked me right into kindergarten class. While this is true, it wasn't by choice. Apparently I had to skip preschool because I got so hysterical the first week that the administrator suggested that perhaps even at four years old, I still needed the confines of home.

From then on I was told I was just a "bag of nerves." My mom and dad would discuss and speculate what made some children easy going (like my cousin Tia) and others afraid of their own shadow (like me).

It was during these preschool flunky days that my mother got a job at Kohl's and arranged to leave me each morning with my Aunt Carol, who lived a few miles away. I don't recall my time there, but shortly after this arrangement Aunt Carol told my parents she could no longer care for me. If any details were offered, I never heard them. My father was especially angry at his sister for bailing, branding her a self-centered, pill-popping drunk who only thought of herself. One might ask why my parents were willing to leave their child with a self-centered, pill-popping drunk, but hey...

I'm currently reading Habit Number 2: "Begin with the End in Mind" in the *7 Habits* book. The idea here is to visualize what you want and go for it. Well, I tried that and so far I've had to cancel one of the two things I wanted to get done today. Although fabric shopping got dashed, my second goal lies ahead of me: Find out all I can about Cole Beckenbauer, the tenth-grade boy who started at Glenview on Monday.

A new student from out of town is big. All I know is his family just moved here from Chicago. At least our cold winters won't be a shocker to him. The bleach bottle White House might be, though.

As I'm heading out the door to school, I see my neighbor, Gerald Zabinski, wheeling his trash to the curb. He waves to me. I wave back but hope to hurry past him so I don't have to engage in conversation. Although I've lived next door to him and his brother my whole life, I don't really know them, which is fine with me.

Gerald Zabinski is a retired dry cleaner with questionable personal hygiene. His teeth are yellow and cracked, and when forced to talk to him, I try not to look at his mouth. His hair is stringy and specked with dandruff. His brother,

August, who looks just as old, has never worked, as far as anyone knows. Gerald told us August has some developmental problems, which we assumed a long time ago. They used to have a nephew, Orin Zabinski, living there, too, but when asked about him, Gerald said he moved to Canada to work in a salmon cannery.

August lives in the basement, at least that's what my parents were told by neighbors. He looks like he bathes more than his brother, but he's not as friendly and seems confused at times. None of us has been inside their house, although Gerald Zabinski did stand in our living room once while my mother wrapped up a Christmas strudel for him.

Since it's third period and I haven't been summoned to the principal's office, I figure it is safe to assume Tyler's teacher accepted his permission slip. Of course, there's the slight possibility my mother was notified and she's just waiting till I get home to unleash.

I take my lunch tray and sit next to Hannah Bristol, the ultimate sophomore class informant. Honestly, truly, this girl is a walking, breathing, live news station. Anything anyone wants to know, Hannah can provide it. And not just headlines, but all the juicy details to go with it. Plus—and it is a major plus—she's rarely wrong. In the unlikely event she can't deliver, she'll find out and get back to you. I'm surprised she doesn't charge for her time, the information so valuable.

Next to Hannah sits Victoria Marsh, a girl so crazy pretty the rest of us secretly wish she'd transfer to Mother Seton Academy, the Catholic girls' school her father keeps threatening to put her in. She's blonde and perky and somehow blessed with the gift of saying the right thing every single time. She's vice president of student council and even volunteers at a pet shelter. She's bilingual—her mother is from Bolivia, and yet Victoria is blond—and claims she never gets into fights with her siblings. How that's possible, I don't know.

It comes as no surprise to Hannah that I, like Victoria, am inquiring about the new guy. His clothes have an edge we've yet to see in Barton, and his dark hair is a perfect blend of messy and cool.

Hannah is leaning over the table, intently chomping down on a turkey-and-Swiss wheat wrap. "He's fifteen, but doesn't have his temps yet—"

"None of us have our temps yet," I say.

"Can I finish please?"

"Sorry."

"He moved here with his mother and stepdad."

"From Chicago," says Victoria. "We know that part."

"Good for you that you know that part," Hannah says.

"He's in my biology class," Victoria continues, unfazed by Hannah.

Hannah looks up from her wrap. "You didn't tell me he's in your biology class."

"I forgot."

"Forgot?"

"So?"

"I'm trying to create a profile here, Victoria."

"What do you want to know?" Victoria takes a sip of her smoothie.

"Did you talk to him?" I ask Victoria.

"No, he's very shy."

"Shy works." I can see Hannah trying to convince herself of that.

She continues talking, but my mind begins to drift. I'm wondering if Victoria ever has bad dreams or if Hannah worries about, well, anything. Are they haunted by things that creep into their unconscious at night? I could just ask them, but then I risk the innocent question in return: "No, why, do you?"

Suddenly something Hannah says brings me back to the conversation. "What did you just say about an investigation?"

"His stepfather is an investigator. That's why they moved here."

"You mean, like an investigator for the electric company?" Victoria does have her moments.

"No, a special assignment."

"What's that mean?"

"There's some top secret criminal activity Barton's finest need help on."

"What kind of criminal activity?"

"You won't believe it. It's right out of *Law and Order*. A cold case."

"Like a murder cold case?" Victoria looks aghast.

"Yes! Right here in Barton. Crazy, huh?"

"I never heard about a murder." Victoria looks doubtful. "Nothing ever happens in Barton."

Victoria's right, nothing does. People leave their car doors unlocked in Barton, some people even their houses. People live in Barton because it's safe. Boring, but safe. So, to hear that a murder—an unsolved one at that—is major news. How did we not hear about this? Of course, all that comes to mind now are my recent dreams.

Victoria shakes her head. "I don't know, Hannah, wouldn't we know about an unsolved murder in our own town?"

Hannah's eyes meet Victoria's with strained patience. "Well, you know now. It's only the details that need to be released."

Only the details. I can feel my heart start to hammer. How much of a coincidence could this be? "Who was murdered?" I finally ask.

"I don't know. Who cares? This is about the new guy, not his stepfather."

Suddenly the room starts to fade. I jump out of my seat. I have to get out, now. I can hardly breathe. *Only the details.*

"Are you leaving?" asks Victoria.

"I gotta go." I grab my bag and push away from the table.

"I'm like so not done," says Hannah. "I have his class schedule, plus his address."

"See ya."

I try to race away as fast as I can without looking like I'm actually racing away as fast as I can. It's not easy.

"You're weirrrrdd, Helen," Hannah shouts after me.

I keep walking, pretending her parting shot at me is a friendly jab, but Hannah means it, and she knows I know she means it. We're not friends, really. She's a necessary contact I keep in my life. I pretend we're friends, and sometimes I almost like her. But other than the local gossip, I know little about her and her about me. Oh, so little about me.

I fear now I've given away too much with my abrupt exit. Not with Victoria but Hannah. Did super sleuth Hannah connect the criminal investigation talk with my rapid departure? She's the last person I need to carry even the slightest suspicion, for if anyone can solve a crime, it's Hannah.

20

Once in the hall, I head for the washroom and lock myself in a stall. I can hear the blood rushing in my ears. I cover them to escape the sound, escape the world and the fate that is following me. What if this Cole's stepfather is here to investigate the murder? Things could unravel in a blink. I mean, how clever could I have been in my cover-up? Not very. Maybe I need to sleep more now, to glean details, fast. As much as I don't want to remember, I need to. If only it were that simple.

This news puts things on a new plane. It could be only a matter of time until this Cole's stepfather is on my doorstep, holding up a small fiber that matches one of my wool cardigans, or a plaster cast that fits one of my knock-off Jimmy Shoo's. They'll take me down for questioning, but I will have no answers. They won't believe me, that I recall nothing. They'll keep me under bright lights in a bare room, trying to trick me into a confession. They'll say they know where the body is so I may as well fess up. I'll ask to see my parents and they'll refuse.

But then again, perhaps if the details of the crime are revealed to me, it will jog my memory and explain who, what, when, and where. There's fleeting comfort in that, to at last know why I did what I did, to stop the running in my mind. But that comfort would be short-lived. I'm not crazy, after all. I'd rather be tortured by the unknown than put in a cell wearing white cotton briefs and an orange jump suit the rest of my life.

I stop and take a breath. I have to function. I have to keep going. It was just a conversation. Maybe it's an old, cold case, like from the 1980s or even earlier. That would exclude me all together.

Maybe Hannah got her info wrong. Maybe Cole's stepfather is just some kind of business investigator, here in Barton to nab a shady accountant cooking the books.

But then again, when was the last time Hannah was wrong?

The rest of the afternoon is a blur. I can barely recall health class and only a portion of English, and only English because it's my favorite subject. We're reading *Hamlet* and are at the part where Hamlet, thinking he killed Claudius, actually killed Polonius by mistake. Poor Hamlet, all he wanted to do was get rid of his creepy uncle, not cause more trouble.

No one understands Hamlet. He was alone. Alone with his thoughts and his madness. I'm starting to wonder if maybe I killed out of defense or, like Hamlet, due to mistaken identity. That could be it. That's a better fit. I mean, I'm not a bad person. I take care of Tyler; I always buy my parents gifts for their birthdays. I even cleaned out the whole garage last summer. (My dad paid me, but still.) Yet, the question remains: Who did I kill?

My plan was to stop by the library after school to pick up a DVD of *Hamlet* I had put on hold (to enhance my reading, not replace it as some do), but I'm skipping the library. I need to get home to something familiar, even if that means looking at the back of Tyler's head in front of the TV. I want to be in my own house and gather my thoughts, figure out what to do.

I walk into the house to the smell of something cooking in the kitchen. At first, I think Tyler must have gotten home early and put the frozen dinner in the oven himself, but then realize the unlikelihood of that scenario. The kid has never turned the oven on in his life. From the hall I can see into the kitchen. My mother is standing there looking at me with a scowl on her face.

"Mom, what are you doing home already?"

"I asked you to put the lasagna in at four o'clock."

"I will."

"It's quarter to six."

"It isn't quarter to six."

"Where have you been, Helen?"

"What do you mean? I came home right after school."

"You did not," shouts Tyler from the living room.

My mother shakes her head. A strand of hair falls in her face. She pins it back. "The lasagna takes two hours to bake. Now we won't be eating till seven thirty."

"Your watch must be wrong. I didn't even go to the library after school." I look at the wall clock. It reads 5:45. School gets out at 3:15.

"I suppose the kitchen clock is wrong, too." She's chopping up lettuce for salad. "And what about Tyler? You know he can't be left in the house alone. He's still a little boy, Helen."

"I don't know how it got so late. I came home right after school."

"You did not," Tyler shouts again. "I was here alone. You didn't answer your cell phone. I kept calling you."

"Tyler never called me." I pull out my cell to look. I would know if my phone rang. I look at it. There are six calls. Five from our landline (that my parents insist on keeping) and one from my mother's cell. My mother grabs my phone and looks at it. She hands it back. "Uh-huh."

I start to cry. My mother puts down the knife and walks over to me. "It's all right, Helen." I notice she looks pretty in her blue sweater. People say I look like my mother, that we have the same green eyes and light brownish hair. I can almost live with the comparison except, of course, she's old.

"Tyler's okay," she says, "but you need to let me know when you're not going to be home. I can't be everywhere."

What my mother doesn't know is I'm not upset because I didn't get the casserole in the oven or because Tyler was alone. I'm crying because there are two and half hours of my day I can't account for. The last thing I remember is leaving school and deciding to skip the library. Even if I had walked slowly I would have been home by 3:40, five minutes before Tyler arrives. So where did the rest of the time go?

I consider telling all this to my mother because it seems like something a parent should know. But this new information, assuming she would even believe me, would probably alarm her to the point of taking me to our family doctor, maybe even the emergency room. And that would result in tests and brain scans and all things scary. I decide to keep the lost time to myself. If it happens again, I'll tell. But for now, I've got work to do. I've got to sleep.

CHAPTER TWO

Of course, now that I actually want to dream, I can't sleep. Two nights in a row and nothing. Nada. Well, almost nothing, just some random half dream that I was someplace with Hannah Bristol and, of all people, Calista Meyer, the girl afraid of her own shadow. In it, Hannah wanted to roast more marshmallows but Calista and I had eaten them all. (In real life I hate marshmallows.) Hannah got so mad at us that she stormed off. Very Hannah.

Since my block of lost time, I've been trying to figure out what happened that day, but like my dreams, I get nothing. I've retraced the steps in my head over and over. I remember the bell ringing and going to my locker because while I was there Ms. Lee from health class walked by and we said hello. And then I remember walking out of school and deciding to skip the library and go straight home. And next, my mother's telling me it's 5:45. I even checked at the library today to see if I had taken out the DVD I had on hold, but I hadn't. I'm disappointed because that would've accounted for at least some of the time.

It's almost lunch period, and to my surprise Hannah and Victoria invite me to eat with them. I thought I may have blown things with my fast exit. My first inclination is to decline. I'm afraid the conversation will turn to Cole, which could lead to his stepfather, which could bring up the investigation of the unsolved murder, which, of course, leads to me. This fear and the possibility that Hannah may grill me on why I left the lunch table so abruptly last time makes me hesitate joining them, but I decide to anyway.

I just realized I forgot to pack my lunch. I only have two dollars on me, so I'll just eat the granola bar I have in my bag. It's just as well because the thought of actually chowing down real food in the presence of Hannah and Victoria today makes me a little queasy.

Victoria is wearing her hair back, which emphasizes her brown eyes, and eyelashes, which are at least a mile long. The girl just never looks bad. It's hard to feel pretty around her. I suspect Hannah thinks so, too, but she would never admit it, not even to herself. Hannah's cute enough with her dark, curly hair and plump lips (she loves to pout them out), but she's not classically beautiful like Victoria.

I attribute Victoria's stunning looks to the fact that she is actually only half American.

People from South America simply have more interesting genes. You rarely see a Latina who looks like she was hit with the ugly stick, but you could never make that sweeping comment about most plain, regular Americans.

To ward off any interrogations, I jump in first. "Any updates on the new guy?"

"You could say that." I swear Hannah looks irritated.

"What?"

"Lucky you, Helen," says Victoria.

"Me?"

"Yes," smiles Victoria. Her teeth are so white they blind me. I want to hate her, it's so unfair.

"Why am I lucky?" (Because they found the killer and it's not me?)

"Because Cole Beckenbauer was just transferred to honors English, that's why. He's in your class now," snaps Hannah, making no attempt to hide her disdain. "So now he's in Victoria's biology class and your English class. I do all the ground work on him, and he's not in one of my classes, not one."

Although I think Cole Beckenbauer is clearly the hottest guy to come along in years, possibly decades, I'm conflicted about being in such close proximity to the stepson of a man who may be making my arrest. My concern is that being in Cole's presence might somehow cause me to look even more guilty than I already feel.

28

"So, you'll see him in class today!" Victoria says.

"Yes, and I won't." Hannah hasn't touched her lunch.

I have a delicate situation here. If I act too pleased, I risk the wrath of Hannah. If I don't act pleased enough, I risk the wrath of Hannah. She's barely recovered from Victoria's news that Victoria shares biology class with him.

I need to let Hannah know I'm no threat in her attempts to get Cole, but I don't want to exactly say that, either. She obviously thinks I have some remote possibility with the guy or she wouldn't be acting so jealous.

The truth is, though, I'm too tired to think about going after Cole. What would he want with a murderer for a girlfriend anyway? When my story gets out, I will be as toxic as nuclear fallout. Let Hannah have him—if he wants her. But let's face it, if he goes for anyone in our squad, it will be Victoria, and Victoria won't even have to try.

"I'll give you a full report, Hannah, I promise," I tell her.

"That means you would have to pay close attention to his every move, Helen."

"I will."

"No, you won't. You always have your face in your tablet or your hand up."

"Sorry, I didn't know paying attention in class was a flaw."

"The point is you can't do both."

"Yes, I can."

"Oh, it's useless."

"It's called multitasking. I can do it."

"As long as you don't fall asleep," says Victoria.

"Fall asleep?"

"Yes, and hopefully you won't snore." Hannah's on a roll now.

"I don't sleep in school."

Victoria shrugs.

"Do I?!"

"You were sleeping in study hall last week. Study hall's not too bad—" Hannah stops. She and Victoria look at each other. "But on the bench?"

"What are you talking about?"

"The other day you were sitting on the bench out front, sleeping," says Victoria. "It was after school. I said 'hi' like three times, but you didn't answer. Fred even tried to wake you up."

"Fred Watson? What was he doing trying to wake me up? Why was he there?"

"We were walking home together."

"Oh, my God, how long did you guys stare at me?"

"Just a couple of minutes."

"Why didn't you just shake me?"

"It wasn't a big deal," Victoria says.

"Not to you maybe."

30

"Helen, why were you sitting on the bench sleeping?" Hannah asks. "Why didn't you just go home instead?" Hannah seems sincerely interested, almost like a concerned friend, which is why I still hang around with her I guess.

I, of course, had no answer. But I did have a question. "What day was that, the park bench?"

Victoria thinks. "Tuesday."

Tuesday. The day I lost time. I remember sitting down on the bench to adjust my backpack. I simply fell asleep. I don't recall the actual nap, but I'm convinced sleep deprivation can do strange things to a mind. I'm so happy I want to jump up and down. I'm not even angry at Hannah for the litany of insults she has just hurled at me.

"I didn't get much sleep the night before. I guess I just sat down and nodded off. Kind of embarrassing, huh?"

"Uhh, yeah. You need to start drinking Red Bull or something." Hannah didn't even see me on the bench that day, so I wish she would shut up.

As it turns out, nothing more was mentioned about Cole, let alone his stepfather. Hannah was so focused on Cole's transfer to my English class that it seemed to suck the life out of further conversation. I'll never know if Hannah noted my panicked exit that day, the day I learned there was a murder investigation in Barton, Ohio.

I spent most of Saturday at the library checking out murder statistics on the criminal docket site online. I chose to go to the library in case either of my parents should stumble upon recent searches on our laptop. I suppose I could always say it was for a class report, but better to be cautious.

I'm only looking into the last five years since I have a hard time believing I could have killed someone before I was ten. I know this is somewhat arbitrary, but I have to start somewhere.

I learned some very interesting facts while researching crime in our county and the four neighboring ones: There is plenty of it. Who knew? Car thefts, domestic violence, assaults, robberies. And murders. Three murders in the last five years to be exact. I also learned that men are more likely than women to kill, that most killers know their victims, and that alcohol or drugs is involved in two-thirds of murder cases.

Of the three murders in our neighboring counties, one was a jealous husband who stabbed his wife, another was a U.S. marine, just home from the Middle East, who snapped after his neighbor borrowed his leaf blower without asking. The third was a convenient store robbery gone bad.

I'm temporarily relieved. Not only don't I fit any of the profiles, they're all closed cases. And even if the murder had taken place farther away, how would I have gotten to that location? The only ones who drive me anywhere are my parents, and I can't see either of them colluding in a murder with their daughter. Yet there are my dreams—the visions—that replay in my sleep. That, and the crushing weight of guilt that is so palpable that at times it's almost unbearable.

The perpetual search for truth in this matter is really a double-edged sword. I want to find out the details; I don't want to know the details. Either way, I lose. Some days I find it difficult to think about the murder, and yet it's when I get to that point that I feel a certain amount of relief because I shut down the thoughts. It's like my mind and body scream *enough!* and it takes a break. It's during these times that I hang with my friends, try to pretend my life is normal. I even talk to Tyler and my parents more during these phases. But the respites are short, anywhere from one day to two weeks, then it's back to my dark reality.

After my Internet search, I decide to stop by my cousin Tia's tattoo shop called Think Ink. It's a few blocks from the library, a small wooden enclave just off the beaten path. I like

Tia's place, and I like Tia. She's the kind of person you feel safe with because she tells things how they are but does it in such a way that you're not insulted.

Tia never gossips, and even though she looks kind of wild with a gazillion tattoos and earrings, she's really a very ordinary person. She listens when you talk, and she can keep a secret. She's also very independent. She opened the tattoo shop herself when she was only twenty-two (last year) by saving up all her money from jobs right out of high school. She took art classes at night and lived at home until she had enough money to leave. Her mother, my Aunt Carol, worships Tia, and if Tia would let her, I think Aunt Carol would move into the shop and work right alongside her daughter. I can't even begin to imagine what that must feel like for Tia to have that kind of status with her mother since I think I mostly irritate my own. Personally though, I find my Aunt Carol fairly obnoxious at times, and off putting, although I would never actually say this to Tia, of course, Aunt Carol being family and all.

On my way to Tia's shop, I decide to stop at a small coffee house a few doors down from her place to pick up a coffee for Tia and a chai for myself. During the week the place is often filled with students from Glenview. I rarely come in here after school because I have to watch Tyler.

While waiting for my order, I notice a bulletin board filled with notes in the hallway by the restrooms. I walk over to it. There's a large printed header which reads: *Nobody Knows...* I begin to look at the small scraps of paper pinned to the board. The first one reads: *Nobody knows... I can't swim.* I look at the next one: *Nobody knows... I love Madison.* Another: *Nobody knows... that I cut.* Wow, anonymous confessions. I'm intrigued and, like a voyeur, continue reading. *Nobody knows... I like boys.* The notes go on. *Nobody knows... I huff. Nobody knows... I'm lonely.*

I pick up my order and walk out. I'm still thinking about the notes I just read. Maybe these writers are hoping someone will hear them at last. I get it.

I open the front door to Think Ink, a cozy space with Tia's mark all over it. Colored lights border the window, and a bright red sofa hugs the wall next to the entrance. Two naked mannequins frame the doorway to the back room where Tia works her magic.

Tia leans against the counter and smiles as I enter. "Hey there, Helen-Melon." Tia has called me that since I was little because I used to eat so much watermelon at family picnics.

"I brought you a coffee."

"You are sooo sweet, thank you." She takes the cup. "This is perfect. I don't have another customer for a half hour."

I sit down on the red sofa and lean back. It feels just like heaven. I could fall asleep in a nanosecond. I wonder if I'd dream in this place.

"So, how've you been, Melon?"

"Okay."

"Yeah?" She sounds as if she doesn't believe me.

"I'm fine, why?"

"You just look a little rough around the edges."

"I do? How?"

"Bags under your eyes. Do you want some cover-up?"

"No."

"You need some."

"I haven't been sleeping very well."

"So, I hear."

I sit up. "You heard? From who?"

"My mother. She said your mom told her you stay up too late on school nights."

"That's what my mother talks about to people?! Did she tell anybody about my winter solstice fabric collage that took me four months to make? Probably not."

"No, but you know how parents are."

Now I'm so angry I want to go home so I can ignore my mother. I worked hard on my collage, hand stitching every minuscule star in place, and all she can talk about are my sleeping habits. Mrs. Kelly, who works with my mother at Fabric City, told me my collage was so good I should enter it in the juried art show downtown next spring.

"I'd like to see your collage sometime. I like the other stuff you've done."

"I'll bring it next time." I love Tia because I know she's not saying that to be nice but because she really wants to see it, because she's an artist herself. She appreciates what's involved in creating something, even fabric collages, which, apparently, people like my mother don't see as real art.

"So, what's up with the no sleep?"

I shrug. There's nothing I would like more than to tell Tia everything—all of it—and just get it off my chest. Tia's so nice I think she might even understand, but I think it's too much to unload on anyone.

"You're worrying about something, I can tell. Is that why you can't sleep?"

"Sort of, yeah."

"It can't be that bad."

I lean back, unable to speak.

"Oh, my God, it is something bad!"

I sit immobile, still not talking.

"Is this about a guy? You're not—"

Now I laugh. "No, no guy or anything."

"Then what?"

"Nothing."

"Are you still afraid the world's going to end?"

"Geez, Tia, I told you that when I was, like, ten."

"Just checking." She comes and sits on the edge of the sofa. "It's okay if you are still afraid of that. I'm not making fun of you."

"I know, but it's not that."

"Good. You're fifteen, you should be having fun!"

I'm eager to change the subject now, for fear I might blurt out something I'll immediately regret. I sigh. "I'm so mad at my mom right now."

"My mother drives me crazy, too."

"Really?"

"Yeah. She hovers over me till I could scream."

"At least she's interested in what you do."

"That's the problem. She has an opinion about everything."

"I didn't know."

"So, you're not the only one whose mother is annoying."

This is the first time I've ever heard Tia say anything negative about anybody in her family. I can think of worse things about my Aunt Carol than nosing into Tia's life. For one, she drinks too much, plus she isn't very nice to Tia's brother, Bass. She named her son after the fish. I mean, who does that? But Bass just seems to keep to himself when he's around, which isn't often. After high school he moved to Pittsburgh and no one sees him much anymore.

Tia's next customer walks in. I stand up to leave. Tia gives me a hug. "I know it's hard for you to turn your mind off once it gets going, Melon, but you gotta try. You look like you're carrying the weight of the world. Talk about it is with someone and then forget about it. If you don't want to talk to me, talk to somebody."

"Thanks, Tia."

"I'm here if you change your mind."

I start back home and get almost as far as the library when I decide to turn around. I walk back in the direction of Tia's shop and stop at the coffee house. I pause near the doorway, then walk in. I move to the *Nobody Knows...* board and look around. I read some of the notes again, then remove a piece of paper from the note pad mounted on the wall and begin to write. I pin it up and look at my post:

Nobody knows... I killed someone.

CHAPTER THREE

It turns out Cole Beckenbauer isn't as shy as we originally thought. He raised his hand in English class on Monday to answer Mr. Silva's question about whether or not we thought Hamlet was crazy. Cole not only answered no but went on to say that the death of a father would cause any guy to act erratically.

"He was angry," Cole said, as if he knew Hamlet personally. "And his mother totally disregarded his feelings after the murder, then married the perp. Who wouldn't be amped?"

Watching Cole dissect Shakespeare with such command made me smile. I didn't have to make a point of remembering what Cole did in class to report back to Hannah; it was imprinted like a brand on my brain. Cole definitely stands out from the others. He doesn't seem to care that he wasn't born and raised in Barton, Ohio, or that girls follow him down the hall before and after school every day.

Hannah is pleased with my report, and because Victoria has no Cole activity to share from biology, Hannah spends most of lunch asking me about Cole. I can tell I've gone up a notch in Hannah's eyes, but the unspoken message is still clear: Don't even think about going after him. What she doesn't know is I won't. I can't. I have much bigger things to tackle.

"Cole's going to the football game Friday night," Hannah announces. There's no point in asking her how she knows this, although I am a little curious. "You guys can both go, right?" She looks at me and Victoria. We nod.

"Let's go early. I want to stake out where he is, and then go sit in front of him."

"Isn't that a little obvious?" asks Victoria.

"Not if it's early. If we go later it would be obvious which is why I don't want to do that." Hannah's getting a little edgy, which makes me think she realizes her plan is a little weak. But Hannah's too thirsty to consider backing down. "Let's go at six. Be at my house by ten of. My mom will drive us."

"That's so early," I say. "No one will be there. And what if Cole doesn't sit down for the game, but just walks around?"

"The earlier we get there, the more I can figure this all out."

Hannah's plan is annoying because it's all to serve her personal goal of getting to Cole. Victoria and I are merely her convenient sidekicks, and once Hannah moves in for the kill, we will be all but invisible.

It's Tuesday and I've yet to go to Fabric City for the new materials I need for my next art project. I plan to avoid my mother when I do go in because I know she will make a point of fussing over my fabric selections. After ignoring her for part of Saturday, she prodded me about my silence until I told her it was clear she's not interested in my work, namely my winter solstice collage. She looked so offended when I said this that I almost felt bad for her. Almost. So now, here she stands in my bedroom ahhing and oohing over my art collage, which makes me want to wad it in a ball and throw it against the wall.

And as if this belated praise isn't painful enough, my mother takes this tender moment to ask me about my bad dreams. I'm so startled at her question that I have to sit down. I've never told her or anyone about my recurring dreams, and certainly not how disturbing they are.

"I don't have bad dreams." The lie flies out of my mouth.

"But you do, a lot it seems."

"Why are you saying that?"

"Because I hear you yell out in the night."

I'm glad I'm already sitting down. "What do I say?"

42

"I can't really make out the words, but you're so distressed. I've come in a few times to check on you, but you're sound asleep."

"Do I do it every night?"

"Lately you have been."

"And you can't make out anything I'm saying?" This is one of those mixed bags. My mother could possess vital information if she can recall any of my actual words, yet do I really want to know? And do I want her to know?

"No, I just hear you shouting out, very upset."

"I didn't know I was doing that."

Suddenly Sheba jumps up on the bed. I pick her up. Her long, gray fur drapes her like a curtain. She's the only one in my house that doesn't bother me. I squeeze her, and she starts to purr.

"It sure sounds like you're having bad dreams."

I shrug.

"Well, something's on your mind."

"Not really."

"You're just so serious all the time, Helen. Is it school?" She's unfazed by my denials.

"No," I say, but then change my mind. "Yeah, maybe. I've got a lot of homework." I'd rather she thinks it's school than go searching for other explanations.

"You've never had problems before. Is it a teacher?"

"No, I just have a lot of work, that's all." Now I want to change the subject because this interrogation will only lead to more lies.

"I can speak to your teachers if that would help."

"No, it's all right."

"Then you need to budget your time better. I know you like going out with your friends and doing your collages, but school has to come first."

"But sewing relaxes me." This is true. The feel of the fabric in my hands, the colors, the threads—they bring a calm to me that nothing else comes close to.

"That's fine, but maybe if you concentrate more on getting your school work done, the night terrors—or whatever they are—will stop. You're scaring your brother."

"I wake up Tyler?"

"Sometimes."

"And Dad, too?"

She laughs. "No, not your dad."

We both know nothing wakes my father. The family joke is he once slept through a tornado—literally. It wasn't until the maple tree out back fell and split the porch rail that he stirred.

"Sorry that I wake you guys."

"It's not your fault, Helen." She stands up to leave my room. "Dreams are just our mind's way of working out our day, that's all."

If only it were that simple.

I'm in a hurry this morning because I plan to stop at the library before classes to free up my time after school. My dad is back in town and can be home early with Tyler. I want to stop by Tia's shop later to show her my solstice collage and discuss my next project.

I put an omelet down in front of Tyler. He stares at the plate. "This has cheese in it."

"It's a cheese omelet."

"I don't want it."

"Just eat it, please. Come on, you do all the other times."

"I want cereal."

I reach across the table. "Fine, give it to me then." I take the plate away and set it in the sink. I grab some cereal and pour him a bowl of Lucky Charms. Actually, the omelet looks good so I take it back out of the sink and join my brother at the table. I notice his head is bent over his cereal bowl. He's separating the marshmallows from the cereal pieces, lining them up on either side.

"What are you doing, Tyler?"

"I like the marshmallows best, so I'm saving them for last."

"Whatever."

"Do you like marshmallows?"

"Nope."

Tyler takes a gulp of his orange juice.

"Tyler, Mom says I wake you up during the night."

"Sometimes."

"Did I last night?"

"Uh-huh."

"I did?"

"Yeah. You were yelling."

"Gee, I'm sorry, Ty." And I am. My little brother should be getting a good night's sleep, and because of me he's not.

He shrugs.

"I don't even know I'm doing it."

I look at him with his freckles and wild strands of hair and I feel bad. He's just one more loss I will have to endure when the terrible truth comes out. And what a thing for poor Tyler to live with. He'll be subjected to ridicule and fights in the school yard, kids teasing him about his sister serving a life sentence for murder at the state penitentiary for women.

Tyler shoves a spoonful of marshmallows into his mouth. "Berry," he says as milk runs down his chin.

"They're berry flavored?"

"No, berry. That's what you were yelling last night."

"Berry? You're sure that's what I said?"

"Uh-huh."

I can feel my stomach start to churn. I'm thinking he didn't hear clearly. My mother said she couldn't make out my words, so probably Tyler didn't either. What could that mean if he's correct? Were there berry bushes near the body? Was I eating berries? Was my victim eating berries?

"Did I say anything else?"

"Just berry."

"It was just a dumb dream, that's all."

The truth is, though, last night I had the same familiar dream with dirt flying and a shoe tumbling down a hill, but with one marked difference this time: I'm positive the shoe is a Nike. Just one shoe. I also saw two limp arms dangling lifeless in front of me. Even in my dream I feel like my head is going to explode. Each time it happens I yell out, although I can't understand what I'm saying. The sounds are deep and low, as if the words themselves are being torn from me. I wake up confused.

"Sleep with the light on," says Tyler.

"I don't know if that would help."

"It helped me when I was little."

I look at him and smile. "Okay, I'll try it, thanks."

Tyler puts on his jacket and backpack while I wash our breakfast dishes.

"Let me know if you hear any other words I say, okay, buddy?"

"Okay. Bye." Tyler walks out the front door.

I'm at the sink doing our dishes. As I place my brother's cereal bowl on the drying rack, it suddenly hits me. Tyler had heard correctly. The word I had said was *bury*.

CHAPTER FOUR

Things are getting messy. Now that I know I narrate my dreams for the entire world to hear, I've got to figure out a way to keep a lid on my late-night talk. What if I say more and my mother, like Tyler, starts to understand what I'm saying? She'll no doubt ask more questions, and I don't know how long I can put her off.

I've got to find out what I'm saying, so starting tonight I'm going to record my dreams. My father has a small voice recorder in the kitchen drawer he never uses, so it won't be missed. It can hold up to 534 hours of recording time which covers roughly two months' worth of dreams.

I head to Tia's after school today with my collage. I've also included a few sketches of some ideas for my next project, a summer solstice arrangement to balance out the seasons.

As I walk by the coffee house, I see it's jammed with students. I notice Hannah sitting with a group of kids, but I decide to skip it and press on to Tia's. As I walk through the door, I see my Aunt Carol's profile behind the counter.

I'd know that head of hair anywhere. It's sprayed and coiffed into a molded plastic wonder. Honestly, she looks like she'd go up in flames if you lit a match near her.

"Well, look who's here," she says to no one in particular, since I don't see Tia anywhere.

"Hi, Aunt Carol."

"Tia's with a client." She walks over to me, high heels clicking on the linoleum as she moves. "How are youuuu, Helen?" She's gushing now, an insincere gesture to be sure, which always makes me cringe. But she's a realtor and can never seem to leave her sales voice far behind. "Are you doing good, hon?"

"I'm fine."

"Are you?" Her vinyl hair bobs slightly as she speaks.

"Yeah."

"Your mom says you've been having trouble sleeping."

"Not anymore." God, I want to kill my mother.

"I was just wondering."

"I was for a week or so. I don't know why my mom even mentioned it."

"Because she's concerned about you, of course. You're always so serious, you worry wart, you."

"I'm fine, geez."

I must have more of an edge in my voice than I thought because she backs off.

"Okay, sweetie."

I notice she has an open can of beer on the counter. Surely Tia would find this tacky and not particularly good for business. I'm surprised my aunt isn't smoking inside, too.

"Is there something I can help you with?" Carol picks up a box from the sofa.

"No, I just stopped by to say hi to Tia." I'm not about to tell her about my art projects, or anything else for that matter. She'd be on the horn to my mother before I even got home. I'm not sure why my mother even bothers with Carol because Carol's not particularly nice to either of my parents. I know my mother doesn't like her much, but she is my dad's sister after all.

"I'll just wait for Tia if that's okay."

"Sure, she shouldn't be too long now." She takes a swig of beer. She sees me looking at the can. "A little pick-me-up. I had a long day showing houses to a foreign couple. They didn't like anything I showed them, not one single house. It's just so aggravating. They're both doctors, too, but you know how foreigners are."

I can't help myself, her shallowness so complete. "No, how are they?"

"You know."

"No, I don't."

"Oh, for God's sake, Helen, you know what I'm talking about. Picky. And cheap. They come to this country with oodles of money and then try to eke out the squeakiest deal they can."

"What's wrong with that?"

"There's something called a commission, you know. It's how I make my living. I have to work. I don't have a husband to support me like your mother does."

I'm pretty sure Carol has just insulted my mother, who I know works at least as hard as my aunt. Carol makes it sound like being married is a matter of luck and so would never include her. The fact is she left Bass and Tia's father when the kids were little. I never heard details of the breakup except my dad used to say the guy escaped just in time, whatever that means. I only met the man once since he now lives somewhere out in California. His kids rarely see him.

"It's always the foreigners who give me a hard time."

"Where are they from?"

"I don't know, Turkey, India, someplace."

"You don't even know which country?"

"No, and I don't care either." She takes another swig of beer.

I notice the box on the sofa is filled with various items. Next to it is a tray of earrings and rings. Carol begins to clear a space in Tia's front window, then places a small vase and some vintage-looking bowl smack front and center.

She then takes the tray of jewelry and places it at one end of the counter, carefully placing price tags on each one.

"I'm kicking things up a bit," she says, trying on one of the rings. "There's no reason Tia can't have a couple of operations going."

Watching my aunt in action makes my own mother look like a saint. Although my mom is sometimes too busy for Tyler and me, Carol is the exact opposite—an explosion of boundary crashing when it comes to Tia. Surely there must be something in the middle.

"I'm stepping out for a cig." She grabs a pack of Marlboros and her beer on exit.

I start to peek into the box of junk when Tia comes out of the back room followed by a girl who looks about Tia's age. "Hey, Melon, what's up?" The girl waves good bye to Tia.

"You have others waiting?"

"No, there's no one waiting." She looks at the jewelry on the counter and shakes her head. "Where's my mother?"

"Smoking out front."

Suddenly Tia spots the stuff in the front window. "What's that crap doing there?!" She quickly pulls the items out of the window.

"Let me see your collage while my mother's still outside. The last thing we need is her opinion."

I quickly unfold my fabric and spread it out on the counter. Tia carefully leans in and examines my work. "Helen, this is beautiful." She runs her fingers lightly across the designs. "This is really good work. I like this better than anything I've seen of yours."

"Yeah?"

"Yes."

"Thanks."

"You've got a great eye for detail. And color. I love these blue strands you've got streaking across the sky."

"That sort of just came to me at the last minute."

"Always go with your instincts. They'll never fail you."

I slip my materials away just as my aunt makes her way back into the store.

"Why'd you take those things out of the window, Tia? Your storefront needs some pizzazz."

"It's junk."

"That's where you wrong."

"It's my place, Ma, okay? You can keep the jewelry here but the other stuff has to go."

"I've been around the block, you know," Carol says as she tosses her beer can into the trash. "I know what people like, Tia. They like trinkets, tchotchkes. This stuff."

Tia just looks at her mother.

Carol gathers her coat and bag. "Okay, call if you need me."

"I will."

"You won't."

As my aunt walks out the door, I wonder how someone as awesome as Tia could have come from the train wreck that is Carol.

Tia moves the boxes to a shelf and sits down. I'm so comfortable with Tia I wish I could stay here at her shop. She looks at me. "How ya doing, Melon? I mean, with your sleep and stuff."

"Not so good."

"I can tell."

"Tia—"

"Yeah?"

I stop. "Never mind."

"What?"

"Nothing. You'll think I'm crazy."

"No, I won't."

"You might."

"You can't be any worse than the rest of us."

"I don't know about that."

"What's going on?"

"Well—"

"What is it?"

I decide to be honest and go for it. "I think I killed someone."

"Oh, my God!" She moves in closer to me. "Like with a car?! Did you take one of your parents' cars out for a drive?"

"No, nothing like that."

"Then what?"

"I can't remember."

"What can't you remember?"

"Any of it."

"Any of what?"

"Of the murder I think I committed."

"Murder?! How is that even possible?"

"I know how it sounds. But I keep having dreams about it and they're so —vivid."

"Oh, dreams! Well, dreams," she says.

"This isn't an ordinary dream. This is a recurring one. It's terrible. I know I lived it. I just know I did. I've felt it for years, although it's just lately that it's nonstop."

"Years?"

"Yes, and it's getting worse. The dreams, I mean. And I see more and more of the story all the time. It plays out like a film. I did it, I just know it."

"All right, let's just look at this logically. You're fifteen. You've believed for years that you killed somebody, which means you would've been a little kid when you did it, right?"

"Thanks, Tia."

"For what?"

"For not laughing at me."

"Well, this is real to you. I can see that. And that's all that counts. It's going to be okay, I promise."

"No, it isn't."

"How could you have killed someone? And how did you get a hold of a gun? Was it a gun you think you used?"

"I don't think so. The picture's fuzzy. I don't have a lot of details except I think I also buried the body."

"How could you do all that without getting caught? Where were your parents?"

"I know it doesn't make sense, except it's so real."

"The biggest question is who, and why? Well, that's two questions."

"I don't know, and I don't know."

"Exactly."

"I'm trying to devise a way to remember everything."

"Why?"

"To get to the truth."

"What you think is the truth."

"Yeah."

"In your dreams."

"Yes. It sounds so dumb when you put it like that."

"You could never kill anybody, Melon. You're not killer material."

"Nobody thinks they're killer material."

"Well, here's what I know: You don't have much to go on to support your theory that you're a murderer, so I recommend you stop thinking about this. Nothing fits. In fact, it really is totally implausible."

"I know."

"Maybe you saw something on TV when you were little that stuck with you. I saw a scary movie about a mummy when I was like—I don't know—six maybe, and I still can't stand anything Egyptian, no joke. I remember almost nothing from my childhood, but I remember that movie like it was yesterday."

There it is. Tia's been patient and oh, so kind, but she doesn't believe me. Not one word. Who can blame her?

I'm walking down the hall at school when Hannah motions to me to come by her locker. She's waving her phone at me.

"Guess what? Just take a guess what I have?" She's bouncing in place now.

"Uh, a new phone?"

"Nooo, but I've got someone's number."

"Cole Beckenbauer's?" An easy guess.

"Yes!"

"What are you going to do, text him? Call him? You haven't even met him yet."

"I know that, Helen. I just thought you might be happy for me that I got his number."

"Oh, I am. That's great. I don't know how you do it, Hannah. His number, that's awesome."

Hannah exhausts me. I always have to figure out how many compliments I need to dole out to her on any given day to keep things balanced. It all depends on her mood.

I can tell she's getting anxious about tomorrow night's game and her plan to sit by

Cole, thinking this is all she has to do to win him over. Like she's the only girl in the school with that idea. Actually, the only one who probably isn't thinking like that is Victoria, and she's probably the only one Cole's got his eye on.

"There's more, but I'll tell you at lunch." Hannah closes her locker. She turns and looks at me. "I like your shirt. That's a good color on you."

"Thanks, I got it—" But she is already halfway down the hall.

We just finished reading Habit Number 3, "Put First Things First", in *The 7 Habits of Highly Effective Teens* for health class. Basically, the idea here is to put things into two categories—urgent and not urgent—then act upon them. I suppose deciding who I killed and how I did it would be under urgent, although I can hardly write that down, so I put *find my necklace*. It sounds safe enough to fly under the radar.

I make my way to the lunch table where the three of us usually sit. Hannah has just announced she's on a no-carb diet. She says she wants to see if she feels less bloated without bread, but it's obvious it's about her plan to reel in Cole. Hannah doesn't need to lose a pound in my opinion, but the girl is unstoppable as we near Friday's game.

"Does anyone want my sandwich?" Hannah holds up a baggie.

"I'll take it." I reach out and grab it. "I forgot my lunch again."

"What are you going to eat?" Victoria asks Hannah.

"An apple."

"You're gonna be hungry," she says.

"No, I won't, and both of you should try this diet, too. I feel so good being off carbs."

"Really?" Victoria looks skeptical.

"Yes, really."

"There's no way I'd give up pizza," Victoria says.

"Me, either."

"It's a small price to pay," says Hannah, nutrition expert.

"No thanks," says Victoria.

"Suit yourself. Anyway, I have some news."

"So do I," says Victoria, smiling.

"About Cole?"

"Yes. He spoke to me today."

I see Hannah's back stiffen. She wants information on the Chosen One, but not to hear that there's been any real communication between her highest competitor, Victoria, and the guy she's marked in the cross hairs for herself.

"So, what'd he say?" Hannah snaps.

"Weird to think we use bacteria to improve our food."

"What are you talking about?"

"That's what he said to me: 'Weird to think we use bacteria to improve our food.' We're learning about how bacteria and yeasts are used to produce foods for human consumption."

"Oh." Hannah ponders this. "When did he say it? Was it to everybody?"

"No, he said it to me as we were walking out of class."

"He said it just to you?"

"Yeah."

Hannah reaches over and grabs the sandwich out of my hand. "Did he say anything else?" She bites into the bread.

"No. Fred was waiting for me, so I went on ahead."

The fact that Victoria preferred to go to a waiting Fred than to continue talking to Cole Beckenbauer obviously lowers Hannah's anxiety level some. Hannah would leave Mohammad at the mountain to speak to Cole, even if it was about the lame topic of bacteria.

I stare at the peanut butter sandwich in Hannah's hand. She tears it in two and hands me half. It's these rare and random acts of hers that cause me not to dump her completely. There's no point in bringing up the fact that she's back on carbs.

"What's your news?" I ask.

"Yes, we're waiting." Victoria looks bored.

"Cole's stepfather is coming to speak at our school."

"He's coming to Glenview?" I ask.

"Yeah, is that fate or what?"

"How is that fate?" Victoria asks.

"I don't know, but Fate's stepfather is going to be at assembly next Friday."

It's finally happened. The moment I have long dreaded. The police know something and they're going to approach us as a whole, ask for tips, information, anything that will give them more leads in the case. They know plenty that they're not saying—that's how cops work—hoping to trip up the perpetrator in some clumsy exchange.

"That's your news?" Victoria asks.

"Yes."

"That's nothing."

"Not when they've asked for student volunteers to help that day. I already signed up."

"And?"

"And you know Cole will be one of the ones up there, too. We'll be together, like a team."

"I'll bet Cole won't be one of the ones up there. I wouldn't if it was my dad," says Victoria.

The student-volunteer angle is throwing me off, unless they plan to fingerprint everyone in the school, then they might need people to move things along. Or use lie detectors, although that seems a bit extreme and like something they might do after they've narrowed down the suspects.

"Really? I'd volunteer if it was one of my parents," says Hannah. "Wouldn't you, Helen?"

I try to find my voice, but nothing comes out. All I see is myself being led away, walking across the gym floor, escorted by a team of police officers to a waiting squad car outside.

"Helen?"

I wonder if they'll handcuff me. Probably, I think that's protocol in an arrest.

"If you're not going to eat that, then I am," says Hannah, taking back the other half of her sandwich.

I will myself to stay and not run off like last time. I can't raise suspicions, especially now, with a mass interrogation coming up.

"Wouldn't you, Helen?" Hannah repeats.

"Yeah, I'd volunteer if it was my dad," I finally say.

"See? Helen would, too," Hannah says. "They want the whole school there."

"What's he speaking about anyway?" Victoria asks.

"I don't know, but we'll know soon enough."

Yes, we will. I want so badly to go home. The thought of afternoon classes plus another entire week of school to get through seems unbearable. Maybe I'll stay home from school next Friday, suddenly sick with the flu. Of course, that might raise even more suspicion with the detective.

"Oh yeah, I almost forgot," says Hannah. "I want you guys to sleep over after the game Friday. And don't say no, Helen, like you always do."

"I don't always say no," I protest, stalling for time. I've got to think quickly because the last thing I'm going to do is sleep over Hannah's and spill my guts aloud in my sleep.

"I'll come," says Victoria.

And then, unbelievably, from my lips I hear: "Me, too."

I think I just shocked my parents with the announcement that tonight I'm heading to bed the same time as Tyler.

"I hope you're not getting sick, Helen," says my mother, putting her hand on my forehead.

What an unexpected boon, handed right to me. "I think I might be," I say. This is perfect foreshadowing in the event I use the flu excuse to not stay at Hannah's.

"Oh, she's just worn out," my father says.

"Worn out from what?" My mother looks incredulous.

"She's a kid, leave her alone, Melanie." My father isn't around much, but when he is I find him much easier than my mother. He's clueless about pretty much everything in our house, but I love him for trying.

"Thanks, Dad. Night, Mom." I run up the stairs.

I practiced setting up the recording device earlier, moving it three times before I finally put it inside the tissue box on my nightstand. I couldn't think of anything to say—so I recited a quote from *Hamlet* that seemed appropriate for the occasion: "Give thy thoughts no tongue."

Now, of course, I can't sleep. I'm thinking about assembly next Friday and the football game two days away. The game isn't a problem but getting out of staying at Hannah's is. I could kick myself for saying I'd go, but Hannah doesn't make it easy. Actually, I don't even mind going to the game; at least it would take my mind off things for a few hours.

As I'm still trying to fall asleep, I hear some noise coming from outside. I go to my window facing the backyard and peek through the blinds. In the shadows I see a man walking slowly around the yard next door. In the faint moonlight I can see that it's August Zabinski. He moves around his yard, kicking dried leaves up in the air as he goes. He rolls an old barrel out of the way, stooping low to the ground to examine the space where it stood. He looks behind bushes, turning in all directions. Suddenly I see the back door open fly open and Gerald Zabinski appear.

"Get in here, August, now," I hear him say. August doesn't move. "Now!" August turns and walks in the opposite direction of his brother, farther into the yard. There's a shed and mounds of mulch and dirt that sit piled high between it and the garage. I can't see much past their shed. Gerald charges down the steps and goes after his brother. He moves fast for an old man.

"I want to see it," I hear August say.

George grabs his brother's arm. "Not tonight." George looks around. "And keep it down, will you? Get inside."

I get back into bed, wondering what August is up to. I lie awhile longer, wishing I would fade off, then realize I must have dozed some because the clock reads midnight. The room is full of pleasant shadows and familiar night noises, which lull me back to a partial sleep.

I see a long, dirt road in front of me. An old woman in a bright yellow sweater is sitting at a picnic bench. It's my Grandma Wren, who died three years ago. She says hello, but then disappears. Now I see a cluster of trees and thick patches of grass below my feet. Suddenly I feel confused and frightened, which jars me awake.

I pull the blankets tight around me. I'm so grateful to be at home and in my bed. I can feel my heart hammering beneath my shirt, and my stomach is queasy. I close my eyes tight, trying to wish the awful feeling away.

"What is this doing in the Kleenex box?" I hear someone say.

I open my eyes to see my mother standing over me, holding the recorder in her hand. I grab it from her. I'm barely awake. "I was listening to some music."

"On that old thing? How?"

"Just forget it!"

"Gee, Miss Crabby, lighten up. I just came in to see how you're feeling before I go to work." She touches my forehead.

"I'm fine."

"Good. I've got to run. Tyler wants pizza tonight. Can you order it? There's money and a coupon on the counter. Half sausage. Get whatever you want on the rest." She starts to leave, then stops at the door. "Oh, Tyler needs help with his rock project. Can you see that it's done?"

"Rock project?"

"He needs to bring in three different kinds of rocks."

"Why can't he do it? It's his assignment. How hard is it to pick up a rock and put it in his backpack? They're all over outside."

"He already has the rocks, he just needs help labeling them. Please, Helen. He has a chart to refer to. He didn't tell me about it until late last night. It's due today."

"Today?"

"Yes. If he'd told me three days ago when he should have, I could've helped him then."

"Fine."

"Thank you, Helen. I appreciate it."

I get up and close the bedroom door behind my mother.

With both my parents gone, I have almost a half hour before I have to get Tyler up for school, although I'd better make it twenty minutes so we have time to do his stupid science project. I get back in bed with the recorder and realize the device is still running, so I press playback. After several minutes of just the sound of rustling sheets and some nasally breathing, I realize I have nine full hours more to wade through. I fast forward and stop, fast forward and stop. Nothing. I'm beginning to feel relieved. Perhaps my bout of jabbering is over. Near the end I press play and hear myself speaking to my mother: *How hard is it to pick up a rock?* I rewind and play it again. *How hard is it to pick up a rock?* I play it again. And again. And again. I don't know why. I just know that I'm drawn to this sentence like a magnet to metal. Suddenly the recorder slips and falls to the floor.

My palms are sweating too much to hold it.

CHAPTER FIVE

Well, there's a first for everything, and getting to a game an hour and ten minutes early is now one of them. Upon arrival we find an empty field, empty bleachers, and concessions stands not yet open. We even have to flag down the guy who takes tickets to let us in, but Hannah is determined to carry out her plan to spot Cole and sit by him. She keeps checking her cell as if Cole himself is going to text her to tell where they should meet.

I'm annoyed that I'm somehow part of Hannah's fantastical plan, but I did agree to it. Maybe things will go as Hannah plans. Maybe she and Cole will hit it off so well I can slip home after the game, unnoticed, which is really what I want to do. That's the perk of being walking distance from the school.

But then there's the matter of sleeping at Hannah's. I couldn't think of any good way to get out of the invitation that I unbelievably accepted (I decided the flu was too obvious) and so will go. Since the second night of recording my dreams came up empty again, I'm less nervous about talking aloud in my sleep.

It's cool for early October, so we're wearing sweaters and jackets. I don't know how Victoria does it, but even in her North Face Denali jacket she looks like a model. This has not gone unnoticed by Hannah, who tends to walk ahead of us both as she scans the landscape in search of her prey. Victoria and I are like two medieval servants trailing behind our master, stopping when she does, moving forward when required.

The stands are filling up now, and people are swarming through the gate. The Glenview Badgers are playing the New Castle Bulldogs. We stop and talk to some girls we know, but Hannah's keen eyes scan the stands and gate, unaware of the conversation going on. The other girls eventually walk off.

"Let's split up," says Hannah.

"Why?" I ask, although I have a pretty good idea.

"To look for Cole. Then text me if you spot him."

"I don't want to," says Victoria.

"Me, either."

"But I didn't know it would be so crowded."

"It's always like this, Hannah," says Victoria.

"Please, please, will you do it?"

"Okay, Helen and I'll walk this way," Victoria says, pointing. "And you go that way."

"Thank you! Text me as soon as you see him."

"If we do."

"He'll be here."

"Are you going to text us if you find him?"

"Of course."

"Yeah, right." Victoria grabs my arms, and we move in the opposite direction that Hannah's headed.

"Finally," says Victoria, laughing, when we're out of Hannah's sight.

Victoria and I walk around, casually scanning for Cole, but with less zeal than Hannah. We pause at the fence while the band plays "The Star-Spangled Banner." The game begins. The crowds are cheering on the Badgers and booing the Bulldogs as the stands fill up. No Cole. Hannah continues to text every few minutes:

Did u find him???

At one point we stop responding. What does she think, that we'd see him and not let her know? Finally, halfway through the first quarter, Hannah summons us to sit with her and some other friends she's found along the way.

I'm beginning to think Hannah's plan has gone awry, just like Victoria and I both tried to tell her it would. Unfortunately, this could make for a long evening at her house after the game. I hope she has plenty of movies in her queue so we don't have to rehash her failed mission all night.

We join Hannah and some others in the stands while the Bulldogs crush Glenview twenty-one to zero as we near halftime. "I'm gonna get a Diet Coke," says Victoria.

"I'm staying here," says Hannah. "Better vantage point."

"I'll go with you," I tell Victoria.

We get our drinks and begin to walk around, this time not looking for anyone; Hannah is on her own.

Suddenly a roar rushes up from the crowd. Ronnie Ortiz has just intercepted a pass and run it down the field for the Badgers' first touchdown of the night. Victoria and I, along with others, rush to the fence to see. In the crush of bodies, I feel an arm press up next to mine. It's Cole Beckenbauer's. I don't know if it's Hannah's constant brainwashing or just simply Cole's astonishingly, hot self standing so close to me, but I suddenly feel I'm in the presence of royalty. "Hi," he says to both of us.

Victoria smiles and says hello in that smooth, flawless way she has, and I'm sure Cole wishes he had brushed up against her instead.

"Hi." It's all I can manage.

"You're Helen Wren, from English."

I'm so startled he knows my name I don't immediately answer him. Victoria elbows me.

"Yeah. You're the new guy. Cole, right?"

"Uh-huh."

"You just moved here from Chicago and you don't think Hamlet was crazy." I can't believe I just said something that inane.

This is about the time Victoria or I should be texting Hannah, yet neither of us makes a move to do so.

Fred Watson, who is standing with Cole, moves over to Victoria. It seems apparent now that he and Cole know each other and may have even come together. Since Victoria spends much of her free time with Fred—she won't call him a boyfriend, though—I'm starting to wonder if Victoria knew Cole would be with Fred all along.

"You ever been to Chicago?" he asks me suddenly. The question throws me, with us standing in a football stadium, surrounded by so much noise and so many people.

"No, I went to Canada once, though. Niagara Falls. So much water." (I cannot believe what's coming out of my mouth.)

Cole laughs. "That's funny. That's good. He's smiling a genuine smile. Somehow he thinks I said something witty, although I can't imagine what.

"Do you miss Chicago?" I ask.

"Yeah."

"I haven't been there—as you know—but I'd miss it. I mean, it's got to be more exciting than Barton."

"Yeah."

"Well, I'd like to tell you there's a lot happening here, but really, there's not." I immediately regret my comment. Talk of Barton could come around to the reason Cole moved here in the first place.

"People are okay here, though."

"They are?"

He laughs. "Yeah. You should know, you live here."

"I haven't noticed."

The four of us move away from the fence and head in the direction of the stands. We take a seat halfway up the bleachers and I see Victoria texting. Within minutes Hannah comes rushing over, waving like she just ran into us, leaping over seats and pushing between Fred and Cole so that she and I are now on either side of him. Fred introduces Cole. Hannah's cheeks are red from the cold, and I'm actually happy (sort of) for her. It's the moment she's been living for. Well, for three weeks anyway.

It turns out Cole is funny and makes us all laugh. Hannah sits there overdoing it, laughing too loud at everything he says, pushing her pouty lips out while he talks. Fred and Victoria are head to head chatting away, which does kind of amaze me. Fred's okay, but compared to Cole he doesn't come close. But no one could be happier about Victoria and Fred than Hannah, who's doing her best to win over the new boy from the windy city.

The game is over. The Bulldogs win twenty-four to seven. We begin to leave when Hannah announces that everyone's invited back to her place to roast hot dogs in her backyard fire pit. This is news to Victoria and me, and I'm guessing to Hannah's mother, too. She gives her address to Cole even though he doesn't drive.

Hannah's temporarily occupied calling home for a ride while the rest of us linger. Fred and Cole will drive together in Fred's car, but Victoria will go with us. Unfortunately for Fred, Victoria's father found out Fred was cited for running a stop sign, then dodging a train at a crossing, all in the first six months of getting his license. Victoria's dad told Victoria she can ride in a car with Fred when hell freezes over.

I'm glad everyone is heading to Hannah's because I don't want the night to end, ever. My fear had been that in Cole's presence I would be reminded of his stepfather and all that implies, but it hasn't happened.

I find Cole easy to talk to, and, once again he finds something witless that I've said funny. I even tell him about my fabric art, and he tells me he used to draw. In fact, he created his own comic book series in seventh grade about flesh-eating aliens from Jupiter who descend upon the Sears Tower in Chicago. No one has read the stories except his friends, but he still has all the copies.

Somehow Hannah manages to pull off the post-game bonfire, all with her mother's blessing. The night has taken on a surreal quality as we sit around the fire in the very cold autumn air.

We learn that Cole has two older sisters, one in college in Nebraska and one married and back in Chicago. He also mentions he snowboards and seems disappointed no one in our group has ever tried it. Fred quickly offers to take up the sport with the first snow. So does Hannah. She's doing her best to lure Cole into her lair, but it's hard to tell if it's working.

An hour or so passes. The fire's dying down. Hannah's mother comes out and suggests that we roast the marshmallows because it's getting late. Hannah's busy in charge of the operation, pushing the white blobs onto sticks and passing them around. She hands me one.

"No thanks."

"Why?" Hannah asks.

"I don't like roasted marshmallows."

"You're weird, Helen. Everybody likes marshmallows."

Suddenly I feel lightheaded, and my ears start to ring. I hear conversation, but it's starting to sound far away. I don't know what's happening. I hope I don't pass out. Could there be anything more embarrassing than fainting in Hannah's backyard with others around, one of whom is Cole Beckenbauer?

All I can hear now is the sizzle of fire and snap of burning wood. I feel like the flames are going to crawl up out of the pit and set me on fire. I start to panic. I want to scream, like in my dreams. I want someone to help me, but I sit immobile, unable to speak. The fear and disconnect is so profound I wonder if it's possible that no one else can see or feel what I do. I force myself to look around. Everyone and everything looks normal.

The laughter and talk gradually become clear again and I feel like I'm back. But although the dark moment has passed, I want to get out of the backyard, maybe even call for a ride home. I casually get up and head for the house. Once inside, I go into the bathroom and close the door. I splash water on my face. I want to go home, but I can't because Hannah will make something out of it.

I don't know how long I've been in the bathroom, but when I come out, everyone but Victoria has left. I realize my window to leave has closed.

"There you are," says Hannah. "We didn't know where you were. Cole said to say goodbye." There's an unmistakable bite in her voice.

I know my job now is to pump up Hannah, tell her I'm sure Cole likes her, that it was awesome and spontaneous of her to have everyone back to the house after the game. This is my script and so I comply. I tell her that Cole must like her or he wouldn't have come at all.

"Do you really think so?" She looks like a beagle waiting for a biscuit.

"Yes, I do, Hannah." I look at Victoria, signaling for her to jump in.

"I can tell he thinks you're nice," says Victoria, without the slightest attempt at sincerity.

"You can?"

"Yeah."

"How?"

Victoria looks at me. "Tell her how, Helen. I can't explain it."

I shrug. "Just the things he said and how he acted around you."

"Oh, my God, you guys are right. I could feel it, too. Oh, Cole, I love you!"

"And now he knows where you live, that's a perk." Victoria seems proud to have come up with this additional comment.

Hannah turns on a movie but talks about Cole through most of it. Victoria has already fallen asleep on the floor. I sit listening to Hannah and wonder how I'm going to get through to morning. After my experience tonight, the hope that I won't talk in my sleep is dashed, which leaves me with one alternative: Stay awake. I tell Hannah I'm not tired and ask her to pick a second movie. She starts one and continues talking.

"He knows my address now," she says. "but doesn't have my number—yet!"

I listen, but say nothing. Cole doesn't have Hannah's number, but he has mine. He asked me for it back at the game.

CHAPTER SIX

Staying up all night at Hannah's proved to be a big mistake. I came home this morning and crashed, not rolling out of bed till two o'clock this afternoon. When I come downstairs, both my parents summon me into the dining room.

"We're worried about you, Helen." My dad sits with his hands folded on the table.

"Why?"

"Your bad dreams." My mom is shaking her head.

"You were yelling and crying up there," says my dad. I can tell from his reaction my mother hadn't mentioned any of this to him before today. "What's going on, honey? What are you dreaming about?"

"Nothing. I just talk in my sleep."

"This isn't talking in your sleep, Helen," my mom says. "This is yelling in your sleep, terror. You sound in serious distress."

"What was I saying?"

"At one point it sounded like hurry, hurry."

"No, no," my father says to my mother. "It sounded more like berry, not hurry. I don't know, maybe it was hurry."

Oh, God, there's that word again. My father is kind of right. It's not hurry, it's *bury*.

"But the point is how upset you were, honey. Mom tells me this has been going on for a while."

"Yeah."

"I'm calling Monday to make an appointment with some kind of therapist," says my mother. "We need to get to the bottom of this."

"I don't need to see anyone."

"You do, sweetie."

"No, I don't."

"Your mother is right, Helen."

"They just put everybody on meds."

"You don't know that. And what if they do? Maybe that's what you need."

"You just want me medicated so I don't bother you guys anymore. I yell in my sleep, so what? You said yourself, Mom, that dreaming is just working out our day. Well, maybe I work out my day loudly! I'm not going to see some stupid shrink."

Things are unraveling. My parents are becoming involved, and if they put a therapist in the mix, the police won't be far behind. I need to talk to Tia. She'll know what to do. She had suggested I try to forget all this, but that was then. Everything's changed now.

I throw on my jacket and leave the house without saying anything to anyone. No one stops me. I walk the mile to town and head toward Think Ink.

I walk into Tia's studio. There are two people on the sofa and I can hear Tia in the back room with a client. I don't want to bother Tia while she's working, so reluctantly walk back out.

I peer into the coffee house, which is teeming with Saturday customers. I go in and order a chai at the crowded counter. I make a point of not looking around because the last thing I want to do right now is make small talk with anybody.

I walk over to the *Nobody Knows...* board. There they are, all the notes, some happy but most sad, confessions from sad people who've been jilted or did the jilting. Lonely guys, angry girlfriends, rejected sons and daughters.

I'm halfway home before I realize I forgot my tea.

CHAPTER SEVEN

Cole and I have been walking out of class together every day this week. It's total bliss. Fortunately for me, Hannah is on the second floor, or I would have a whole lot of explaining to do.

It's kind of a surprise Hannah doesn't know more about Cole and me—little that there is to know, really—but maybe she's too focused on snagging him for herself to see clearly. Her next strategy in the Cole saga is to try to pair up with him at assembly on Friday. According to Hannah, as it turns out, Cole is part of the assembly volunteers.

The fact that the school hasn't announced what this assembly is about adds to my belief that it's something big and very serious. I could easily ask Cole about it, but I can't even think about that event now, just two days away, let alone speak of it. If my fears about Friday are correct, everything Cole thinks he knows about me will come crashing down like a crater. I just want to enjoy the brief time I have with him.

I struck a bargain with my parents, although my mother isn't too happy about it. I promised I'd talk to my guidance counselor at school about my disturbing dreams if she would hold off calling a therapist or our family doctor.

"It's not the same," my mother said when I proposed my plan to her.

"I know, but I really like Mrs. King, my guidance counselor. I think she can help."

"I'm not convinced of that, but I'll give it this one time. I need for you to be honest with her about what's going on, though."

"I will, promise."

I'm seeing Mrs. King today during my lunch period. I plan to be honest, meaning I won't directly lie; I just won't volunteer too much. I'll say enough to keep my mother happy while I figure out what to do about, well, about everything.

I'm actually glad I'm not eating lunch with Hannah and Victoria today. The closer we get to Friday, the harder it is to sit there and act normal. Plus, yesterday bordered on painful with Hannah going on about her imagined future with Cole. I feel guilty that I've been talking to Cole and not sharing that information with Hannah, so conditioned am I to report back to her.

I've really only talked to Mrs. King a few times before, once to do with being placed in honors classes, and the other when I had to get permission to take senior art. Now that I have to speak to her about something personal, I want to walk right past her door, but I don't.

Mrs. King is a tall, pretty, African-American woman who always wears matching dresses and shoes. She owns an array of suits in various colors, and thus, shoes: violet, red, mustard. Today she has on a teal jacket with the same shade of suede pumps. She smiles and tells me to have a seat. We make small talk for a few minutes. She even offers me a mint from a bowl on her desk, which I decline. We discuss my grades, which she's pleased are holding up. I'm sure she's wondering why I'm in here if everything is so fab.

"So, how's everything else going, Helen?"

"Fine."

"Are you sure?"

"Uh-huh."

"Your mother tells me you're having nightmares."

Of course my mother called her. She was afraid I wouldn't tell Mrs. King the truth. "I am," I mumble.

"Can we talk a little about them? See if we can sort things out a bit?"

"I really don't want to."

She goes on about getting enough sleep and how things we don't even think might be bothering us really are. We talk about classes and friends and other seemingly innocuous topics, but then it's back to me.

"Are you having trouble with any of your classmates?"

"No."

"No one?"

"No."

She looks at me, then leans forward so that we're almost face to face. "You're safe in here, Helen. I want you to know that. You can talk to me."

"I know." And I do know. I feel safe with her. She's very kind. Part of me would like to just dump the whole thing out, right here, right now. What a relief that would be. But I'm sure she would be obligated to do something with the information I impart. I can't take the chance.

"Do you feel safe in your home?"

"Yes."

"Is there anything going on there we should know about?"

"No."

"Do you feel you're in any danger?"

"No, nothing like that. I know what you're implying, but there's nothing, really."

"I'm not implying anything. I'm just trying to help you figure out what's going on."

"I just talk in my sleep, that's all. My mother's making a big deal out of nothing. She wants me to go to a therapist, which I don't need, so I asked if I could come and see you instead."

"And I'm glad you did. You're always welcome to come and talk to me, but I may not be the one to help you with this problem, Helen. Your parents might have a better plan."

"I doubt it."

She sits back in her chair and takes a quiet breath. She's so calm; I wish I could be like her.

"Are you being bullied here at school?"

"Bullied?"

"Yes, bullied."

"No!" I'm insulted by the question. I think of the Calista Meyers as the ones who get bullied. It's the weak, the disabled, those who can't stand up for themselves. "The creeps that bully don't pick on people like me."

"What's 'people like you'?"

"I don't know."

"Exactly, Helen. You have no idea how much bullying goes on here. It's not just the ones you would imagine. There is a lot of behind-the-scenes cruelty around. It's a real problem."

I'm genuinely surprised at this statement. I know about a few incidents, but our principal, Mr. Jenkins, made such a big deal out of it when it happened that I thought it was rare and that it was other schools that had the problem, not Glenview.

"In fact, it's so prevalent," Mrs. King continues, "that we're having a special assembly about bully prevention on Friday."

"You are?"

"Yes. We have a whole program planned."

"The assembly is going to be about bullying?"

"That's right."

Nothing else Mrs. King asks or says to me after that registers. I'm so relieved I want to jump up and hug her. Cole's stepfather is coming here to talk about bullying. Not homicide. Not cold cases. Not arrests.

I cut the fabric pieces for my summer solstice collage and lay them out on a long board next to my sewing machine. I place the yellow and burnt orange sunset against the backdrop of a pale blue summer sky and trace the horizon with a single thread of metallic gold, giving the appearance of shimmering water. I sit back and imagine myself in the peaceful scene, wishing I could step into the story, with its soothing colors and simple lines. I add pieces of green paisley print for grass, and gray-shaded remnants for tall trees.

I work slowly and methodically. The process becomes a working meditation, a tactile mantra as I move the fabric pieces around to form a pleasing tableau. Then, without thinking or planning, I pick up a patch of brown and place it to the far right in the scene. I place a piece over it, shaping crude pieces layer after layer. I'm not sure why I'm doing this; I'm drawn to it somehow.

There's a knock at my bedroom door. Tyler enters, holding something in his hand.

"I just wanted to show you my paper. I got an A on my rock report."

"That's great, Tyler." I look over his work.

"Mom said to show you since you helped me."

"You did most of the work. Hey, Ty, remember when you heard me talking in my sleep before?"

"Yeah. You were doing it again."

"I was? When?"

"Last night."

"Do you know what I was saying?"

"You were calling Tia."

"Tia, really? Are you sure?

"Yeah."

I'm glad it was Tia's name I said. It makes sense since I told her my story.

Tyler heads for the door. "You should sleep with your light on, like I told you."

"That's a good idea. I will."

It's not every day I take advice from an eight-year old, but what have I got to lose?

My mother's still home this morning, downstairs fixing breakfast. When I walk into the kitchen, Tyler's whining.

"But I have a warm sleeping bag, Mom."

"It's October. It's too cold, Tyler."

"No, it isn't."

"You guys will be banging on the door at three in the morning for me to let you in."

"No, we won't."

"Forget it. You should have thought up this scheme in July."

"What's going on?" I ask.

"Tyler and his friend Ethan want to camp out in the backyard. I told him it's too cold."

"It really is, Tyler," I say.

My mother puts an oatmeal muffin and a sliced apple in front of Tyler.

"I've never camped, but I think it would help to have some of the right gear, Ty," I tell him. "Maybe Dad can take you sometime when it gets warm."

My mother sets a plate down in front of me, too. "Thanks, Helen," she says, referring to our brief alliance. "Actually, you did go camping once," she says. "But I'm sure you were too young to remember."

"We did?"

"You did, with Aunt Carol and her kids when you were about three." She pauses. "I must have been crazy to agree to that," she says, half to herself.

"Aunt Carol pitched a tent?"

"I doubt it. Bass and Tia probably did," she says with a faint smirk. "All right, finish up your breakfast, you two. It's almost time to leave."

We're at the part in *Hamlet* where Hamlet refuses to tell anybody where he's hidden Polonius's body. He hadn't intended to kill

Polonius; he thought it was his stepfather, Claudius, behind the curtain. Well, Polonius shouldn't have been standing there. I'm not saying he deserved to be stabbed, but things happen when you put yourself in harm's way.

This may be a first for Hannah, but it turns out she was wrong about Cole being one of the student volunteers at assembly. This means she won't be sharing the stage with Cole after all. She's now forced to sit through assembly handing out brochures. She doesn't even try to disguise her disappointment. Cole sits in the bleachers along with everyone else.

Our speaker, Jonathan McCreedy, begins by talking about the practice of bullying, from cyber bullies to one-on-one school yard thugs. He shows a power point with some unpleasant photos and gives examples of how some kids' lives have been ruined by the cruel actions of others. You can hear a pin drop as he talks. I have to believe that Cole is proud of him.

Cole asked me if we could meet up after school because he has something to show me. Yes! I'm so glad I don't have to rush home to be with Tyler today. We meet up outside the main door after school and walk two blocks over to the library. I tell him how much I liked the speech. He says his father travels to schools across the country to talk. I notice he refers to Jonathan McCreedy as his father. My curiosity is burning now.

"Is he your father or stepfather?"

"He adopted me when I was seven. I think of him as my dad. My real father died when I was five. I kept my father's last name, though."

"Why do you call him your stepfather if he's like a father to you?"

"I don't call him that. You guys do."

It's true. It was Hannah who first reported that it was Cole's stepfather. She had her information partially right, but no one ever challenges her on her data or her sources. Everyone just simply believes Hannah.

We sit on a sofa by a window in the back of the library. Cole opens a large envelope and pulls out some materials. "These are my comic books from seventh grade that I was telling you about."

The books are amazing. His artwork is sharp, edgy, almost professional looking. I flip through them, and we stop and read short sections together about flesh-eating aliens of Chicago.

"You're the only person I've shown these to since I was twelve."

"They're awesome."

"Yeah?"

We get drinks from the vending machine and talk more about aliens, drawings, and then about my fabric art. We talk about Chicago and what it's like to move to a small town after living your whole life in a large city. I can't imagine what that's like, I tell him, since I personally find Barton so uninteresting. He misses home, he finally admits. And although he has an amazingly positive attitude about starting over, I can tell, in spite of his humor, he doesn't feel he fits in all that much at Glenview.

The incline is steep. Mounds of cracked dirt run along the descent. I see someone in a dim light through the trees but can't make out who it is. There's shouting. Suddenly there's a thud. It's a blunt sound, followed by a low groan. I see two limp arms dangling. The hands are large. A man's hands. The weight of his body is more than I can handle. A white Nike shoe falls and hits the ground with a thud. It tumbles down the embankment before I can catch it. I run and run. My chest is burning. It's dark and I stumble.

I open my eyes. My little brother is standing next to my bed, looking at me. I glance around. It's morning. I've knocked the things off my nightstand and torn off the covers. All that remains is my pillow, which lies lengthwise on my body, like the lid to a crypt.

"I'm sorry, buddy, just a bad dream." I try to sound nonchalant.

Tyler just stands there. We remain like this for a long moment. I, looking up at the ceiling, and Tyler looking down at me. He reaches over and takes my hand. "It'll be okay," he says.

CHAPTER EIGHT

I need some advice, fast, so I call Tia at work. Seeing Tyler's face this morning made me realize I've dragged the most innocent of innocents into my trawler net, and I can no longer justify continuing to do nothing and hope for the best. It's time to stop running. I hope Tia can help. She tells me to come by at one o'clock.

First, I make a list of all I can recall about my dreams.

<u>IMAGES</u>
Trees/Grass/Hill (or cliff)
Nike shoe
White shirt
Grandma Wren (in yellow sweater)
Dangling arms – man's hands?

<u>SOUNDS</u>
Shouting or laughing
Thud

<u>ACTIONS</u>
Lifting
Running/Stumbling

I read over the list. Nothing more resonates so I put the notebook in my bag to show to Tia this afternoon.

Hannah texts me that she and some other girls are going to Synder's Circle, a collection of stores and restaurants which is the closest thing Barton has to a town center. I'm glad I can't go because it's getting more and more difficult to be with Hannah. She thinks her barbecue sparked the beginning of something with Cole, plus made her and me closer friends, which couldn't be farther from the truth.

I stop in the coffee house for a chai before going to Tia's. I look at the *Nobody Knows...* board and see my note. Suddenly I'm horrified. What was I thinking?! This is a written confession. I'm lucky the owner didn't turn my note over to the police. I quickly rip the paper down and throw it away.

As I walk into Think Ink, I see Tia standing at the counter. She looks up and gives me a sheepish smile. Sitting on the sofa is my aunt, sporting a new head of hair and a can of beer. She and Tia are eating burgers from Wendy's.

"I didn't know you were coming or I would have picked something up for you, Helen," says my aunt.

"It's okay."

"How's your mother doing? "

"Good. She's one of the fabric buyers at work now."

Carol brushes crumbs off her pants. "And your dad? How's that brother of mine doing? You think he'd give me a call once in a while."

"He's busy. He's gone a lot."

"Sounds like it."

"I had a dream about Grandma Wren the other night," I say suddenly, although I'm not sure why. I guess because Grandma Wren is family to all of us.

"A nightmare?"

"Geez, Ma," says Tia.

"No. It wasn't much of a dream, really, but I saw her sitting at a picnic table with a yellow sweater on. She looked nice."

"I remember that sweater," says Tia. "Do you, Ma?"

"Yeah." Carol looks pensive now and I'm wondering if I've made her sad by bringing up her mother.

"Sorry," I say.

"Nothing to be sorry about." Carol gets up to throw her container in the trash. "She's dead. That's the way it works. You live, you die."

I get up. It's obvious Tia and I can't talk. "I've gotta go. I just stopped by to say hi. I'll see ya."

"Later, then, Melon."

Tia texted me later and we plan to meet at the coffee house on Wednesday.

I've been trying to figure out a new way to handle Hannah and I think Habit Number 5 from our *7 Habits* book might be of some use: "Seek First to Understand, Then to be Understood." The idea here is if we listen with the purpose of understanding another, we begin true communication.

For all Hannah's jabbering, I think she's scared of not having friends. Tomorrow at lunch I'm going to try to steer us away from the subject of Cole. It'll be friendly and positive. Maybe Victoria will even join in. She and I are both tired of hearing about Cole. The Cole that lives in Hannah's head, anyway.

Mr. Silva thought it would be interesting to act out the scenes from *Hamlet* today, so he calls on the willing few and assigns roles to the rest. We're at the part where Claudius has put a hit out on Hamlet, but crafty Claudius orders it to be done in England, not Denmark, where everyone is watching. He puts Hamlet on a boat, but fortunately Hamlet is smarter than the two henchmen and he knocks them off first.

I know Hamlet is a killer, although oddly I don't hold it against him, maybe because most of the murders can be justified. Sort of.

Cole waits for me at the door after class and asks if we can meet somewhere after school. I tell him I have to go home to be with Tyler.

"I'll just walk with you to your house, then, if that's okay."

"Sure, but that's out of your way."

"It's okay, I'll meet you out front then?"

"Great."

I'm walking down the hall to health class when I pass Mrs. King. She has on a bright tangerine wool suit with matching Mary Janes. She stops me. "How are you doing, Helen?"

"Much better, Mrs. King. It really helped to talk to you. Thank you," I lie.

"I'm glad. You come and see me anytime. I mean it." She continues on down the hall.

Cole is waiting by the north door when I come out. I would love for him to come over, but my mother is adamant about anyone being over when no one's home. Cole is grinning. "I've got something to show you."

"What?"

"You'll see."

"What? Tell me. What?"

"I started another book."

"That's awesome."

"It's kind of a retread."

"You mean with the aliens?"

"Yeah."

"Show me."

"I'm updating one of my old ones," he says.

"Let me see it." I tug at his backpack, and he dodges me, laughing. "Come on!" I continue to pull at the straps of his bag.

He starts to spin around and around so I can't get to his backpack. I keep circling him, trying to pull it from his shoulder. We're both laughing now. Then, suddenly, in my peripheral vision I see someone off to my right. I turn. It's Hannah, staring at us.

"Hey, Hannah." Cole throws her a nod, completely unaware of the fantasy world Hannah lives in with him.

Hannah turns on her heels and sprints off before I can say a word.

"What's with her?" Cole asks.

"Bad day, I guess."

My mother brings home a pattern and materials for a pirate costume for Tyler for Halloween. She asks me if I would make it for him since I sew better than she does. It's true I'm a better sewer, but I'm ready to take the allowance I get for watching Tyler and go buy him one off the shelf at Target. But my mother will protest and I don't need the battle. At least I have three weeks to make it.

I decide to lay out the fabric and pin the pattern for Tyler's costume now. This task isn't nearly as relaxing as working on my collage, but I'm too hyped up after the Hannah encounter today to concentrate on homework anyway. I tried texting her, but she's ignoring me completely. So much for Habit Number 5.

As I'm working at the dining room table, I hear my mother on the phone with my dad, who's in Indiana. "Where does she think we'd get that kind of money? We're not giving her a cent, Dale. We're not. I don't care if she is your sister."

My mother, clearly agitated, walks back through the dining room. I'm about to ask her about the phone call when she holds up her hand to stop me. "It's nothing." That nothing is Aunt Carol.

I'm in the school gym sitting inside a large sail boat with a group of kids, talking. Suddenly Cole shouts "Look out!" and I see Hannah balanced high up a mast about to throw a rock at me. I duck and it misses. I run outside and my Grandma Wren is standing there. "I'm sorry, Helen," she says.

Tia is already in a booth when I arrive at the coffee house. Before I can say anything, she starts in.

"Arggggg, Melon," she says, holding her head in her hands. "My mother has no money and wants to move in with me."

"Wow," I say. I wonder what Tia would think if she knew her mother had asked my parents for money.

"She's going to do it. I mean, I can't very well tell my own mother no when she has no money and soon no place to live."

"How'd she get so broke?"

"The housing market tanked with the economy, plus she's bad with money. But never mind, we're here to talk about you."

"I know what you said before about none of my dreams making any sense, but things are getting worse. I was hoping you could help me sort this out."

"How?"

"There's a pattern to my dreams, and they're getting more intense." I reach into my bag. "I've made a list of the important and recurring things. Look." I hand it to her. She reads over the list but doesn't say anything.

"What do you think?" I finally ask.

"I don't know, Melon," she says, looking at the list again.

"Grandma Wren seems to be the only one who's actually talked to me. I think she's trying to tell me something."

"This all kind of creeps me out."

"Sorry."

"You've got to stop thinking and writing about all this dark stuff. Bodies and dead people. It's not healthy."

"But it's what's going on with me."

Tia takes a sip of her coffee. "Maybe," she says without looking at me, "you should go see someone."

"Like a psychologist?"

"Yeah."

"My mom already said that."

"Maybe she's right. You can't go on like this. It's not because I think you killed anybody, because I know you didn't, but because these images are so disturbing. It's going to get to you, Melon."

What Tia doesn't know is, it already has.

CHAPTER NINE

Hannah walks right past me in the hall before classes. I call to her, but she keeps going. It's been a week since she saw Cole and me outside school. Who knows what story she's conjured up in her head. I have to keep reminding myself that I did nothing wrong. Should I not talk to Cole or be his friend because Hannah has some distorted notion that with time Cole would lay down his life for her?

I'm closing up my locker when I see Hannah heading straight toward me.

"Some friend you are." Her voice is thick and salty.

"Hannah, can we talk?" And at this moment I realize I really want to. I'm tired of skulking around.

"You're a total fake." Her eyes are fixed and hard.

"What are you talking about?"

"You pretend to be all innocent and sweet, but deep down you're just a phony. You're all about yourself and nobody else."

"That's not true, Hannah. And I know this is about Cole and me and what you think you saw."

"I know what I saw."

"You saw us talking outside of school, that's it."

"Plus, the two hours you spent at the library the week before. And you walk out of class together every day, he walked you home last Monday, and you guys text each other all the time. You gonna deny that, too?"

I don't know who Hannah's mole is, but the person is good. Hannah can't possibly be working alone, otherwise she would have confronted me sooner. Her sources must have wanted to collect enough data to give her an accurate report of Cole's and my activities before she pounced. This means all those times at lunch when she casually asked me about Cole and I blew her off, she knew I was lying. She's been behind the scenes, crouched in the bushes, waiting for the perfect time to move in. She didn't accidentally run into Cole and me that day; it was planned.

"Cole and I talk, so what?" I'm angry now.

"It's more than that and you know it." She's speaking between clenched teeth.

"I'm not in your way. Go after Cole if you want. Nobody is stopping you."

Hannah's face flushes with anger. "This isn't even about Cole and me!"

"What?" I'm actually a little confused now.

"I don't care if he likes me or not."

"Yeah, okay, whatever."

"I don't!" Spit flies from her mouth. She's so high key now that I look around to see if anyone is watching.

"Cole is the one person you haven't been able to control, and it's killing you."

"Shut up, Helen, just shut up!" She moves within inches of my face. I can feel her breath on me.

"I guess this was never going to end well, with you and me," I say.

"You got that right."

"Hannah, come on."

"You'd better watch your back, that's all I can say."

"Is that a threat?"

"You bet it is. Your day's coming." She kicks the locker next to mine with the heel of her boot as she continues on down the hall.

I watch her until she turns the corner. It's like I just witnessed an encounter with the evil twin of Hannah Bristol, not that the other Hannah is that fabulous. I knew she would be upset, but the rage rising out of her is something I never saw coming. Totally savage.

I'm angry, yet I'm glad Hannah finally knows, because that means I can speak freely to Cole without worrying about what she would say. She probably won't ever talk to me again, but that's all right. And to think Cole has no idea the drama that has unfolded around him today.

Cole texts me after dinner to ask if I'm going to the football game on Friday. He and Fred are going, and he suggests maybe we can all meet up. I'm already picturing it: no Hannah, which leaves Victoria and Fred and Cole and me. It sounds like a perfect night. Beyond perfect.

I'm about to text Cole back when my mother comes into the living room to remind me Friday night is my father's birthday dinner at Smokey Joe's Rib Palace. I swear this is the first I've heard about it. I can't believe I have to sit through a family dinner when I could be at a football game with Cole.

"Can't we go to dinner Saturday or Sunday? Dad's birthday isn't until Sunday anyway."

"No, we can't go Saturday or Sunday. I've had this planned for a month. I reserved a table for nine at Smokey's."

"Nine?"

"Yes, I invited Julia and Dave, plus the Westons from Dad's office. And Aunt Carol. Tia can't make it."

"Great."

"And I ordered a double-dark chocolate torte from Frattori's, too. This dinner means a lot to your dad, Helen, so just buck up."

I'll have to text Cole back that I can't go to the game. I wonder if Hannah will be there. And if they are all there, I wonder if she'll head straight to Cole. Probably.

I'm almost through with the pirate costume for Tyler. I decided to get it out of the way so I can concentrate on my fabric collage.

I have Tyler try it on so I can see if the pants are too long. I tie the red sash around his waist and button the jacket up. I walk across the room to get a better look at the pants. Tyler's so excited to have the costume on that he grabs a poker from the fireplace and jumps up on the sofa. "Yarrr, scurvy dogs," he shouts, and lifts the fire poker high over his head, about to bring it down on a sofa pillow.

"STOP!" I scream loudly. "STOP IT!"

Frightened, Tyler quickly drops the iron rod.

My mother rushes in. "What happened?!"

"Nothing," says Tyler.

"Is anyone hurt?" My mother's out of breath.

"No," I say.

"Helen freaked out for nothing."

"Helen, what happened? Why on earth were you screaming?"

"He was swinging the fire poker."

"At you?" She turns to Tyler. "Were you swinging that at your sister?"

"No, she was standing way over there." He points to the other side of the room. "I didn't do anything!"

My mother comes over to me. "You scared me to death, Helen. Honestly, I'm still shaking."

Tyler rips off the costume and throws it on the floor, then runs out of the room. I follow him into the kitchen. He turns his back to me when I come in.

"I'm sorry, Tyler."

He doesn't respond.

"It wasn't your fault."

"Why'd you get so mad?"

"I don't know."

"I wasn't gonna hit you."

"I know. I'm sorry, really. I don't know why that bothered me so much, Ty." I pause. "So, do you want to play a video game?"

He spins around. "Yeah!"

Tyler knows I'm groveling now. I almost never agree to play video games with him, let alone suggest it. "I get to pick the game," he says. "I'll pick two, no, three games."

"Don't push your luck."

Tyler's already at the computer. He eagerly walks me through Angry Birds: Star Wars. He's winning, too, of course. He's an amazing gamer, and not just for his age.

We're now halfway through Minecraft when I start thinking about my latest dream. Then, out of nowhere, the image of Hannah high above me comes into focus and I see what she is has in her hand: a rock.

And it's with this image that it becomes clear. The thud I heard in my dream the other night was the thud of a rock. I shudder to think what the rock hit to cause the blunt sound it made, a sound that still resonates with me now, even in my waking hours.

CHAPTER TEN

Victoria and I haven't spoken of the drama with Hannah, mainly because Victoria has gone on record as one who likes to remain neutral. I am starting to wonder, though, since she continues to eat lunch with Hannah, a table at which I'm obviously no longer welcome. I eat with some of the girls from my health class at the other end of the cafeteria. So, I'm glad when today Victoria stops me after lunch, asking if we could talk for a minute. She pulls out her phone.

"I just want you to know how much this upsets me."

"What does?"

She hands me her cell. "This text from you to Hannah. Hannah just forwarded it to me."

I read the text:

> R u going 2 game fri? hope
> V isn't. does she put u 2 sleep
> 2. Idk y Fred's with her.

I'm stunned. It's so obviously nothing I wrote. Clearly Hannah's done this. She may as well have signed her name.

"I didn't send this text. I would never write anything like this about you."

"It's forwarded from your phone, Helen."

"I see that, but I didn't send it. This has Hannah written all over it. You know Hannah. Look at it. She's trying to get you turned against me with a stupid trick."

"How'd she send it from your phone then?"

"I don't know."

"The message was sent at ten-thirty this morning."

I think a minute. "I was in history. Maybe she had someone take my phone out of my bag and send her the text."

"Without you knowing it?"

I don't say it, but I agree it's hard to believe because my bag sits on the floor by my feet. I take out my phone. The text is there, sent at ten-thirty, just as Victoria says. Am I losing my mind? Has it finally happened? But it makes no sense.

"I don't know how she did it, but she's obviously behind this. She has spies all over the school."

"Spies?"

"Yes, how do you think she gets so much dirt on everybody?"

"Spies and sneaking your phone without you knowing? Do you know how paranoid you sound?"

"Victoria, I have no reason to say anything bad about you. I would hope you know me better than that. Don't you think it's an awfully big coincidence that this text popped up now, right when Hannah's on the hate trail with me?"

She thinks for a moment. "Come up with how she managed to text from your phone and I might believe you." She walks away. Guilty until presumed innocent.

Pirates seem to be popping up everywhere. Hamlet's managed to get himself captured by a couple after the two hit men from the boat are bumped off. And then for a ransom, the pirates return Hamlet to evil Claudius. Things are starting to look grim for Hamlet. Mr. Silva assigns the final scenes of the play for Friday, but I think it's safe to say there'll be no happy endings in Denmark.

Cole and I walk out of class together and he tells me how disappointed he is I can't go to the game Friday. That makes two of us.

"Fred told me about the text you sent Hannah," he says.

"The one where I'm supposedly trashing Victoria?"

"Yeah."

"Hannah's such a liar. I didn't send that text. I don't know how she did it, but Hannah's behind it. She's trying to pit everybody against me."

"Why?"

"It would take all day to explain."

"Did Hannah get a hold of your phone?"

"I don't know."

"Weird."

"Yep."

We reach the end of the hallway where we part directions. I look at him. "I hope you believe me."

"I do." And he does.

Ms. Lee waves me up to her desk at the end of class and tells me there's a message in the office for me. I can't imagine what it is, so I head straight there. The main office secretary, Ms. Zehnder, walks over to the front desk. "Helen Wren, correct?"

I nod. She's rifling through some notes on her desk. Why would they call me down here with a message?

"Is everything all right?" I ask.

"We got a call from someone a few minutes ago who said she was your mother. She said to tell you she was getting out of work early and you wouldn't have to be home to watch your brother."

"My mother called and said that?"

"No, someone pretending to be your mother. That's why you were called to the office. The message sounded suspicious, so we contacted your mother at work. And, as we thought, she hadn't placed the call. This is clearly a prank. Do you have any idea who would have done this?"

I think for a moment. I'm not trying to figure out who did it; that part's obvious. What I'm trying to decide is weather to throw Hannah under the bus. If she finds out (and she will) that I gave her name to the office, what else will she do? If I let this go, maybe she'll just stop.

"No, I don't know."

You sure?"

"Yes."

"This isn't funny."

"I don't think so, either."

"We don't tolerate this kind of thing at Glenview." Her tone is accusing, like I'm somehow in on the prank.

"If I find out who it is, I'll tell you right away."

"I would certainly hope so."

For all Hannah's savvy at dispensing news and ability to control the minions in her squad, her attempts to trip me up are pretty substandard. Did she really think she (or her peeps) could pull off impersonating my mother and no one would question it?

I sit through my last class of the day brooding. The more I think about what Hannah tried to do, the angrier I get. Well, the gloves are off. At the sound of the last bell, I rush to Hannah's locker. I know Cole will be outside waiting for me, but first things first. Hannah turns and stops when she sees me.

"Really, Hannah?" I get in her face. "First the text and then the call?"

"I don't know what you're talking about. And get out of my way. I need to get into my locker."

"I don't know how you did the text thing, but you'd better tell Victoria I didn't send it."

"Of course you sent it. That's why I showed it to her. It's time she knows what kind of a person you are."

I'm so mad my mouth is like cotton. I don't feel very brave, but I refuse to move. "Tell Victoria. Now!"

"There's nothing to tell her."

"And quit involving my family in your stupid pranks." Now I'm the one speaking through clenched teeth.

"I don't know what you're talking about." She has a smirk on her face that makes her pouty lips look rubbery and distorted.

"Yes, you do." I walk away from her, my knees shaking.

"You're a freak, Helen Wren," she yells out.

"And you're a liar!" I shout back.

Cole's waiting for me outside. I walk right past him when I see him. "Come on," I tell him as I keep moving.

He has to walk fast to catch up with me.

"What's going on?"

I tell Cole everything, starting with his first day at Glenview High and Hannah's relentless reconnaissance missions, ending with our argument and her subsequent prank. I even tell him about the football game and Hannah's plan to sit with him. He doesn't have much of a reaction to any of it.

"Did you have this problem with girls in Chicago, too?" I ask, trying for some levity.

"Not that I know of."

I tell him how I confronted Hannah at the locker and how she denied everything.

"You need to give her name up."

"No way."

"Yeah, you need to."

"She'd just make things worse for me."

"She's already doing that."

"It's fine."

"It's not fine. She's involved your family."

"I just don't want to think about her right now."

We've almost reached my house when I see August Zabinski standing in our front yard, peering toward the back. He has on a long, mangy fur coat and fur hat. He looks like something out of an old Russian novel.

"Pardon me, excuse me," he says, bowing slightly as we near him. I notice he's wearing white running shoes like his brother Gerald always does. The shoes look odd with the fur coat and hat. Well, August is odd. "Just lookin' for somethin'," he says. He bends down and picks up some stones and slips them into his pocket. "Lost these before."

Suddenly there's the sound of a key turning in the lock of his front door. August darts off toward the back of his house before the door opens. Gerald Zabinski steps out. "Hello," he says with his yellow smile.

"Hello, Mr. Zabinski."

"Beautiful fall day, isn't it?"

"Yeah."

He seems preoccupied and moves into his yard, looking around and down the driveway. I assume he's looking for his brother.

Tyler's bus hasn't come yet, so Cole and I sit on the front steps.

"What are you gonna do about Hannah?"

"I just want to ignore it for now. I need some time."

"I know what you're thinking, that she might quit, that this stuff will go away, right?"

"Yeah."

"But it might not. And stuff can spread. Things that go viral can destroy you."

I'm already destroyed, I want to tell him.

It's foggy and I see my grandmother approaching. "I'm sorry, Helen," she says. "You were so little." I ask what she's sorry about. "There was nothing you could do," she says.

Nine of us are sitting around a round table at Smokey Joe's, and all I can think about is I could be at the football game with Cole. But maybe that wouldn't have worked out so well in light of the latest drama.

I wish Tia was with us, but who can blame her for having "other plans." Except for Tyler and me, it's a table full of boring adults cracking lame jokes about hair loss and crow's feet. My aunt is slugging down draft beers as fast as they bring them.

My mother, who doesn't get out much, is more chatty than usual. I hear her talking to Julia Arbright, a family friend, about the woes of child rearing and how Tyler wants to camp out this weekend in our backyard.

"I didn't know Tyler wanted to camp out," says my father, who's always about two weeks behind with everything family.

Tyler perks up. "Mom says I can't."

"Why not?" my dad asks my mother.

"Because it's late October, Dale."

"So what? Ty's tough. Sounds like fun."

"Yes!" Tyler's almost leaping out of his seat.

I'm thinking about the night I saw August Zabinski wandering around his yard after dark and wonder if I should mention the incident in case Tyler and Ethan actually do sleep out there.

"Can we talk about this later, Dale, and not at your birthday party?"

"You're the one who brought it up, honey," says my father.

"I was talking to Julia."

"Well, it's out there now."

"Can I still camp out?" Tyler looks worried.

"We'll see, son," says my father. He looks at my mom.

"He's eight years old, Dale." My mother is trying to stay pleasant. "Are you going to sleep out there with him and Ethan?"

"I don't want Dad with us!" Tyler looks aghast.

My father ruffles Ty's hair and laughs. "So you don't want your old man out there with you?"

My mother shoots my father a dirty look. "It's a good thing it's your birthday," she says.

"Yeah, good thing, huh?" My father winks at her, which seems to make my mother more annoyed.

An uncomfortable silence falls over the whole table, and I see the birthday soiree heading south, fast. My mother turns to Carol.

"Speaking of tents, I was telling Helen the one and only camping trip she went on was with you and your kids when she was little. It must have been something because Helen's never wanted to camp since." My mom gives a little laugh.

"That sounds vaguely familiar," says Carol.

"Of course, Carol, when Dale and I went to Boston, remember?"

"Oh, yeah, yeah." Carol takes a swig of beer.

"Where did we go camping? Around here?" I ask my aunt.

"I don't remember. I'm surprised I went at all. My kids must have really nagged me."

"It was Blackfoot Springs," says my mother.

"That's right. We went canoeing." Carol wipes her fingers and mouth with a wet nap. "The boat wouldn't stay upright. I paddled like crazy." Carol picks a piece of rib meat from her teeth. I'm tempted to fetch a toothpick from the lobby for her.

The waitress comes out carrying the chocolate torte with lighted candles and places it in front of my father. My mother jumps up and hustles Tyler and me to my father's side for a picture with him and the cake.

As the waitress serves cake around the table, I watch Carol with her bouffant bat's nest and acrylic nails and wonder how Tia can stand it, living with her. Poor Tia. I guess we all have our crosses to bear. I heard that once in Sunday school.

CHAPTER ELEVEN

Nothing like finding a random skull rolling around the dirt of a newly dug grave. Not only does Hamlet find a human head, but he learns the head belonged to an old friend. And if that isn't enough, the new grave Hamlet's looking at is for Ophelia, his former love interest who went off the deep end (so to speak) and drowned. And I thought I had problems.

I'm looking at the back of Cole's dark blue sweater in class while I listen to Mr. Silva, but mostly I'm thinking about Hannah and how I dread every single day now, for fear she will say or do something sinister and destructive. She hasn't, but the lull is making me nervous. I suspect something's brewing, kind of like the eye of a hurricane. I pass her in the hall once a day and see her in the lunch room, but we don't make eye contact.

I see Victoria on occasion. She mumbles hello as she passes, but the frost coming off of her could chill a sauna. I still can't believe she would take Hannah's side in all this, knowing what Hannah has shown to be capable of in the past. Even Fred ignores me. I know this makes it awkward for Cole since they are sort of friends, but to Cole's credit he defended me to Fred and Victoria on more than one occasion.

Sometimes I wonder if the stall in activity from Hannah means she's called off the dogs. Maybe, but I doubt it because Cole and I have been spending even more time together, something which would definitely not go unnoticed by Hannah and her spies. The biggest breakthrough with Cole and me is that my mother said he could come over our house when she or my dad was home. I think my mother is secretly pleased because she's the one who suggested Cole come over some weekend day, which he did last Sunday.

My parents at least had the decency to just say hello, then exit to another room. Tyler, on the other hand, asked Cole if he wanted to play a video game. Cole accepted the invitation before I could intervene, but I told Tyler it was one game only, then he had to get lost.

I still can't believe Cole Beckenbauer was in my living room for a whole afternoon. I showed him my winter solstice collage, and we talked more about his plans to expand his new Chicago alien series. We made chocolate chip milkshakes in the kitchen, and for one brief moment I forgot about the dark cloud that hangs over me. If only things could stay like they were that one afternoon.

My mother lost the battle with my dad about Tyler's campout and so the boys take their sleeping bags and head to the backyard. They dive into the tent my dad pitched for them earlier in the day. (My mother made Tyler wear long underwear and promise to keep the lantern on beside them all night.)

It is two a.m. and forty-one degrees outside when my mother decides to wake my father and tell him it is his turn to stand post.

My parents don't know it, but I am wide awake myself. I look out at the tent from my bedroom window and see the pale light of the lantern reflect the boys' shadows. The whole idea of them out there makes me strangely uneasy and, like my mother, I wish the boys would come inside.

In a switch of events, I get a text from Tia asking if I could meet up with her sometime this week. We're meeting today at three o'clock at the coffee house.

Tia's already sitting down with a coffee when I arrive. "Thanks for meeting me here, Melon," she says. There's not much bounce in her voice.

"Is this about the dream list I made?"

"Dream list?" She looks confused. "No, I just wondered if maybe you could help me with my mother."

"Me? How?" Oh, I hope I'm hearing wrong.

"Well, actually your parents. I thought maybe they could try talking to my mother. It's horrible, Melon. She's been in my apartment two weeks and I'm going nuts. I have no privacy, as you can imagine."

"How awful, Tia."

"She says she's looking for a job, but she's not. She watches TV all day or comes to the shop. I finally told her she had to quit coming there. She's bad for business. She started making suggestions to people on what they should get. One guy walked out."

"Gee, but what can I do, Tia?"

"I thought maybe you could tell your parents how bad it has gotten. You know, and maybe they would lend her some money so she could move out. I would talk to your mom and dad myself, but I think it might be better coming from you since I'm not close to either of your parents."

I'm thinking back to the phone call where my parents argued about lending Carol money. I feel I'm in the middle of something now, without even trying to be.

"What about Bass? Did you talk to him?"

"Yeah, but he doesn't care. He thinks if I can't stand it, I should just move, like he did."

"Oh."

Tia stirs her coffee. "Listen, you probably don't know this and I shouldn't be telling you, but one of the reasons I want to ask your father for money is because I know when Grandma Wren died, your dad inherited all her money. I know it wasn't a lot—she and Grandpa obviously weren't rich—but I remember hearing things like 'what a nice little nest egg for Dale'."

"But there's just the two of them. Grandma must have divided the money. Maybe she did and your mom spent it all."

"No, that's just it. My mother and Grandma Wren had some big falling out before she died and she left everything to your dad."

"How do you know?"

"My mother was going on about it one night a few years ago. She's very bitter about it, as you can imagine."

"What was their argument about?"

"I don't know."

"Maybe it isn't true."

"No, I'm sure it is. My mother wouldn't lie about that."

"I wonder if my parents know why."

"More things for you to find out."

I find this information all very unsettling. Why wouldn't my dad have just given half of the money to Carol anyway? But Tia's wrong if she thinks I'll be able to find out anything. "I don't have a lot of credibility with my parents, Tia. My mother doesn't take me seriously at all, ever, and my dad's not home that much. It might be better coming from you. I can be there with you when you talk to them."

Tia's face falls. "Oh, Melon." She clearly doesn't want to approach my parents herself.

"Okay, I'll talk to them," I quickly say. "But I have to warn you they'll not only want to talk to you themselves, but they might actually tell your mom about all this."

"No! Oh, no, she'd make my life totally miserable if she thought I did that. More miserable than it already is."

"Well, I can tell them you don't want your mom to know, but there's no guarantee they'll be quiet. I'm just saying. I know my parents."

"Oh, this can't be happening." Tia throws her head back. "What am I going to do?"

"Would it be so awful if your mother found out you were trying to help her?"

"She would know I was just trying to get rid of her. It wouldn't be pretty."

"Okay, well, let me think about how to do this."

"But they can't tell my mother I went to any of you. Promise she won't find that out. Tell them how important it is. Just give them enough information that will help."

"Okay."

"Thanks."

As I watch Tia I realize for the first time that, in spite of all appearances, Tia is afraid of her mother.

She stands up. "Come with me." She motions me to follow her. She heads for the *Nobody Knows...* board. When we get there, she points to a pink post-it note. *Nobody Knows... my mother is driving me crazy.* We laugh. "Big surprise who wrote that," she says.

Just as we're turning to leave I spot another post. It's in heavy black marker on a green piece of torn notebook paper. I can barely focus my eyes. It reads: *Nobody Knows...Helen Wren killed somebody.*

Tia doesn't see it and continues on towards the door. "You go on, Tia," I call out to her.

I look around and quickly rip down the note.

Well, I was right about one thing: It is just the eye of the hurricane.

CHAPTER TWELVE

My life is spiraling out of control, fast. My secret is out and it's not going to end with a simple note in a coffee house. I won't even turn on my cell or the lap top for fear of what is on there. There's no doubt in my mind that Hannah is behind the note, but what I need to do is figure out how the information got to her. I make a list.

<u>POSSIBLE SOURCES</u>

1. Spy saw my post and told Hannah.
2. Hannah herself saw me post the note.
3. Spy overheard Tia and me talking.
4. Tia told someone (and it got back to Hannah).

The last one on the list is very painful to even consider because I don't believe Tia would ever tell anybody anything, but at this point I can't , eliminate her. Everyone is under suspicion.

I know now I have to tell Cole my whole story before Hannah sends everything out on Twitter if she hasn't already. I'm about to call him when there's a knock at our front door. It's Cole. My mom lets him in and we go into the family room, as far away as I can get from Tyler and my mother. I shut the door.

"I'm glad to see you," I say.

"I should've texted you."

"My phone's off anyway."

"I heard some stuff and I wanted to come over here and tell you myself."

"I know what it is."

"No, this is bad stuff."

"That I killed somebody?"

"You do know!"

"I assume Hannah's texting and tweeting everyone."

"No."

"She's not?"

"She's playing it smart. This is serious stuff and she knows if she leaves her own trail through texts and tweets, it can be traced back to her and she could be in a lot of trouble. Word of mouth is safer. It's harder to figure out who started the story."

"How'd she do it then?"

"Hannah told Victoria that she heard it from somebody. Victoria told Fred, Fred told me. Someone will start tweeting and this'll go viral. It probably already has."

"None of it matters anymore. Hannah's just getting started."

"Are you ready to tell now? What more do you want her to do? She's crazy, Helen. You gotta start by telling your parents, then school, and go from there. If she can say you killed somebody, where will it stop?"

"What if it's true?"

"What if what's true?"

"That I killed somebody?"

"Yeah, okay." He looks almost amused.

I know from this moment things will never be the same in my life. I don't know what the future holds, but I know the secret I've been holding is no longer a secret.

I tell Cole everything. Every dream, every fear, every memory, the recorder, the *Nobody Knows...* board. I'm so resigned to my fate that I deliver this with little emotion. It's as if I'm running down an inventory list for a warehouse.

But like Tia, Cole doesn't believe my story either, at least that I killed someone. He dismisses it so easily, I'm almost annoyed. He says I'm too nice to hurt anyone and my thoughts are way irrational. I suppose that should be some consolation, except all that means is the shock will be that much greater when the truth comes out.

I guess I should have assumed Cole wouldn't accept such a wild notion, but I'm glad he at least knows. And I feel now that the truth is out there, Hannah can't do anything else to me.

"You'll figure all that out, your dreams and stuff. What you've gotta concentrate on is getting Hannah off your back."

"I'll talk to my parents this week. My dad will be home Friday."

"That's two days from now. That's too long."

"It doesn't matter."

I walk him to the front door. He starts to leave. He turns to me. "It's gonna be okay, Helen."

I walk back through the dining room toward the kitchen when I see a stuffed, life-sized dummy propped up on a dining room chair. I let out an involuntary scream. I hear my mother and Tyler laugh from the other room. "I see you found Tyler's dummy," my mother's voice trails in. "Isn't it good? Tyler and I made it for the porch for Halloween."

"It doesn't have a face," shouts Tyler.

I look at the large featureless figure that Tyler has dressed in a white shirt and a pair of my dad's jeans. It has on rubber boots and a baseball cap. It starts to slide off the chair, so I grab it to stop it from falling. There's a loud clunking noise as it hits the edge of the dining room table. I reach around and feel a large pocket my mother must have sewn into the back and filled with several large sized rocks to give it weight for sitting.

Suddenly and without warning I feel like I'm going to be sick. I throw the dummy down, which slides to the floor as I run from the room. A surge of heat rushes up my neck and to my face. I go into the bathroom and sit on the edge of the tub, hoping the nausea will pass. I find my body beginning to tremble. It's as if something has taken over my senses and I've stepped outside of myself.

As I sit in this quiet disconnect, I see the image of a rock before me, the same image I saw weeks earlier when I was with Tyler at the computer. It's a large rock, and I see it as clearly as if it's a photograph before my eyes.

I close my eyes and see a man in a white shirt with his back to me and the rock raised high over his head. With one swift, deliberate blow, the rock comes crashing down on his head. He lets out a groan. Blood gushes from the gaping space like a red, running stream and spills onto his white shirt. The rock comes down again with a thud, followed by the cracking sound of splitting bone. The man crumples into a heap. I feel myself run as fast as I can, consumed with sheer terror at the horror. I can feel myself trying to gain speed and my chest burns as I move.

I realize I'm now on the bathroom floor and for a brief moment I have no idea if I'm awake or asleep, alive or dead. I smell death and blood and dirt all around me yet I'm fairly certain I'm lying on the cold tile, awake. I feel I'm floating in another universe and that if someone doesn't anchor me soon, I may not be able to get back.

I remain on the floor, shuddering. I can feel my heart beating so hard that I place both hands on my chest as if this gesture will somehow slow the pounding beneath my sweater. I take the cotton bath mat and wrap it around me. I close my eyes and with as much courage as I can gather, I try to stay with the image. This is the portal I have been denied until now, but this time I'm stepping through.

I begin to replay the abhorrent image of the rock smashing the man's skull. I force myself to stay with it. The man's back is to me. He's sitting with his head bent. I think he's sitting on a large rock. I hear another voice but see no one. The man responds in a low tone, but I can't make out his words.

I see a pale light by a tree and realize it's a lantern that's illuminating him. I wish I could see his face. I scan the scene with my mind's eye and see trees and thick brush. There's a rocky ravine off to one side, which seems to hollow on the curve. I stay focused on the surroundings and the intermittent silence.

I hear shouting and crying. The shouting isn't coming from the man, it's from someone off in the shadows. Suddenly I see the large rock over the man's head, and it comes down with a thud. The man in the white shirt isn't moving.

I think I've stopped breathing for several seconds. My body has gone rigid and I think this paralysis is happening in real time, on my bathroom floor while I'm reliving a real scene.

The long, heavy arms dangle like a doll's as his legs scrape against the dirt. More crying. Some moaning. Is the man moaning? Dear God, is he still alive? I move quickly and one of his shoes falls off and rolls down an embankment. I can't catch it. I realize it's so dark now, I can't see anymore. The light has been extinguished.

I begin to sprint. I feel myself running as fast as I can, breathless with fear. My mouth opens to scream and I don't know whether the words are released into the air, but I hear them in my head as I bolt. *Bury, bury,* I mumble to myself. It's dark where I am now. I have to think which way to go. I stumble and fall to the ground. I hit my knee. Suddenly there's darkness and quiet as I continue to rush forward. I think I'm calling to someone, but I can't be sure. Then, stillness.

I hear a thumping in the distance and try to make out the sound. "Helen? Are you okay?" It's my mother knocking on the bathroom door.

"I'm fine."

"You're not sick, are you?"

"I'm doing my eyebrows."

"Well, hurry up, Tyler needs a shower."

"Just a sec."

I get up and slip out of the bathroom and into my bedroom. I grab my journal and begin to write what I recall from the incident just played out in my head.

One thing I know, it wasn't a dream back in the bathroom. The story was real and came tumbling out in sequence, played out as it clearly once happened. Dreams are jumbled stories. This was a memory and it came back to me in replay, frame by frame.

I feel like Hester Prynne from *The Scarlet Letter* as I walk into school today, a marked target, but the first thing I notice is that people aren't staring at me as I thought they would be. It seems eerily normal. But I believe this can be attributed in part to a theory put forth by Madalynn Flores, a girl in my art class.

Madalynn, like many, read a tweet that says I'm headed to death row for murder, but because the idea is so outrageous she thinks nobody's taking it seriously. Fake news. Maybe if I'd been accused of shoplifting or a back-alley drug deal they'd have something to work with, but murder? No way, says Madalynn.

If only they knew.

I carefully considered Cole's advice to go to our principal about Hannah, but I've changed my mind. I've decided not to, yet, partly due to Madalynn's theory, but also because of my parents. The thought of bringing them into this unnerves me beyond anything.

Plus, and I know Cole strongly disagrees with this, but I have a hard time believing Hannah can be stopped. I can't prove any of the things she's done, plus she obviously has a posse of faithfuls out there helping her. It would take a federal undercover sting to get to Hannah. And what's left? She's exposed me to the world, even if people don't believe the story.

When I arrive home to wait for Tyler's bus, I notice my mother's car's in the driveway. She isn't supposed to be home until five-thirty. I walk in the house to find Gerald Zabinski standing in our kitchen with my mother, who's holding my cat, Sheba. It's an odd sight at three in the afternoon.

"Mr. Zabinski brought Sheba home." My mother's petting Sheba's head.

I'm confused because Sheba has a cat door to the outside and comes and goes as she pleases.

"I'm afraid my brother, August, threw a rock at your cat, and it stunned her, so I picked her up and brought her home. I'm sorry about that."

Stunned nothing! If Sheba let Gerald Zabinski pick her up, she must have been almost knocked out or injured, otherwise she would have clawed and bitten any person other than someone in our family who tried to carry her. My mother knows that, too. I grab Sheba out of my mother's arms.

"Why did your brother throw a rock at my cat? Sheba doesn't bother anybody."

"Helen!"

I ignore my mother and keep my eyes fixed on Gerald Zabinski.

"The cat was strolling around our back yard. August is very protective of our property, as you know."

"He could've really hurt her. Maybe she is hurt."

"She's fine, Helen," my mother says. "I looked her over."

"You can't tell if she's in pain."

Gerald seems nervous now, and my mother shows him to the door. She walks back over to me. "That was very rude, Helen."

"The guy throws a rock at Sheba that could've killed her and you're yelling at me."

"Oh, stop exaggerating."

"Why are you defending those men?"

"What would you like me to do, call the police? Gerald Zabinski was honest enough to come over and tell us what happened. He does the best he can with his brother."

I pick up Sheba and head to my room. I want everyone to leave me alone, everyone except Cole and Sheba. The poor thing hit with a rock. The irony of this is not lost on me, except Sheba seems to be in one piece, unlike the man in my dream.

I take out my summer solstice collage and spread out the pieces I've cut and place them on the fabric. Sheba jumps up and stretches out in the center of the fabric.

"Sorry, Sheba, you've got to move." I pick her up and set her on my bed. I run my fingers along the lines I've sketched on the cloth and notice the fabric feels moist and sticky. I look at my finger. Blood. I follow the trail on the fabric.

I go to Sheba and run my hands over her body. On her right side, beneath a matted mass of thick fur is an oozing wound, the blood soaked up by her dense coat. I part the fur and see a small, torn and open wound where August Zabinski struck her with a rock, ripping open her soft flesh. He must have hit her with considerable force.

I feel such rage, I want to scream. I hold Sheba to me and feel her low purr and moist breath on my neck. I cry at the injustice and indignity she's suffered, an unwarranted blow delivered with no warning.

The vet irrigates Sheba's wound before sewing her up. She suggests that the rock, if indeed it was a rock, must have had a sharp edge in order to cut her open the way it did. I ask what it could have been if not a rock.

"A sharp piece of metal, a knife maybe," she says.

"A knife?!" I'm stunned. It was the only thing I could manage to get out of my mouth.

My mother, annoyingly, says nothing about the doctor's comments, but does announce that she is very relieved that the veterinarian wants Sheba to stay indoors for the next ten days. It's because it gets August off our backs for awhile, I'm sure, although she would never admit that.

After dinner, I hear a text come in. It's from Tia.

Anything?????

It's brief and in code, but it's loaded. She's inquiring about whether I've gotten anywhere with my parents about her problem. I'd forgotten all about it. I go to my mother.

"Did you know Aunt Carol moved in with Tia?"

"What?!" My mother actually puts down the pan she's drying.

"She lost her job and her apartment, so I guess she has no money."

"That's Carol for you."

"It's probably hard for Tia."

"I'm sure it is."

"I wish we could help."

"No, we're not giving her any money in case that's where you're going with this. Grandma Wren left Carol enough money so that she and her kids wouldn't ever have to be in this bind."

"She did?"

"Yes. It wasn't a huge amount, but if Carol had been careful and made smart choices, she'd be all right today. Plus, Grandma Wren did so much for Carol after she got divorced, helping out with Tia and Bass while Carol bounced from job to job."

"I didn't know that."

"This isn't stuff for you to worry about, Helen. But I guess it's no secret Carol gets under my skin."

Obviously I believe my mother's version of the story. It just makes more sense. Tia, on the other hand, believes my aunt.

This is one time I don't look forward to seeing my cousin.

CHAPTER THIRTEEN

I don't want to text Tia that the mission with my parents was a colossal failure, so I head to Think Ink today to tell her in person. Tia's at the counter when I come in. She looks so happy to see me that I already feel guilty. I get right to the point: "It didn't work."

"Ohhhh."

"Sorry, Tia, I tried." I feel like I'm throwing my parents under the bus now, making them look bad for refusing to help their own family. But the only other choice is to tell Tia what my mother said about Grandma Wren's money, and I'm not about to do that.

"You were my last hope, Melon."

"There's always hope."

"I'm not so sure about that."

I'm not so sure, either. I guess it's just something people say to each other.

For our homework assignment, Mr. Silva tells us to select a favorite quote from *Hamlet* and write its meaning, so I choose a line from

Polonius in Act Two: *Though this be madness, yet there is method in 't.* Polonius thinks Hamlet's crazy yet admits Hamlet still has some good points. Things aren't always what meet the eye, that's for sure. For example, Polonius thinks Hamlet's upset over love, but really Hamlet's just faking the crazies to plan revenge for his father's death.

I'm not sure exactly when it happened, somewhere between discussing Act V of *Hamlet* and sitting in study hall, but suddenly it hits me, out of nowhere. A discovery. A big one. I can't wait to tell Cole.

I text him to meet me at the library right after school. I arrive before him and search the perimeter of the library until I find a fairly large-sized rock. I see Cole walking toward me at a fast pace.

"Put your backpack down," I say as he approaches. I'm jumping out of my skin.

"Okay." He places his bag on the nearby bench. "What's up?"

"You'll see." I hold up the rock.

"What's that for?"

"You'll see. Okay, in my dreams I have the image of the rock as clear as a photo in my mind, remember?"

"Yeah, that's what you said."

"I always see the rock raised above the man's head."

"Yeah."

I hold up my arms to demonstrate. "I see it raised high like this. Then it comes down on the guy's head."

"So, are you planning to kill me or what?"

"Ha, ha. Sit here on the bench. I'm going to come up behind you with the rock and pretend to hit you on the head with it."

"Okay."

I lift the rock high in the air and come down close to his head. I shudder. "You okay?"

"Yeah." He laughs.

"I'm going to do it one more time in slow motion." I raise the rock high over Cole's head and come down again, stopping just before his head. "Okay, let's change places now."

He moves around to the back of the bench. "Are you gonna tell me what you're doing?"

"Soon, I promise."

I give him the rock and sit on the bench. He comes up close behind me.

"Tell me when you're ready to hit me on the head."

"I'm ready."

"What are you looking at?"

"What?"

"Right now. Where are your eyes focused?"

"On the top of your head."

"That's where mine were focused, too, on the top of your head."

"That's where they would be, on your intended target."

"Exactly."

"In my dreams I see the rock raised high in the air, every time. The rock. I see the rock."

"Not the head."

"Never the head, always the rock, high in the air."

"If you'd been the one holding the rock, you'd have been looking at the guy's head, not the rock."

"Yes!"

"So what you've been seeing is from an observer's point of view."

"Yes. Do you know what this means?"

"What I knew all along: You didn't kill anybody."

"Right."

"What's more likely is you witnessed something bad, really bad, a long time ago."

A shift in perception and clarity can happen in a nanosecond. I know, because it just did. I hadn't realized there had been a ten-thousand-pound weight sitting on my shoulders until it was lifted. I feel so light I could fly. The sky looks bluer, the October leaves crisper and for the first time since I can remember, I feel genuine hope.

"I have more good news," says Cole. "I don't think you need to worry about Hannah anymore."

"Why?"

"One of her key spies, Chloe Lodge, got mad at Hannah this morning and told the office Hannah was the one who made the phone call impersonating your mother. Then, another of her peeps caved after watching Hannah freak out on Chloe in the hall. And—get ready for this, Chloe is also the one who sent the bogus text about Victoria."

"Chloe! Of course. She's in my history class. I can't believe she did that."

"Everyone's talking about Hannah now. Not a loyal bunch. Anyway, I'm guessing Hannah will be laying low now that her house of cards is falling."

And I thought the day couldn't get any better.

CHAPTER FOURTEEN

Since believing I didn't kill anybody, I thought the dreams might let up, but it's turned out to be the opposite. Something is working its way out of my mind, and I need to step aside and allow it to come forward. I go over and over last night's dream:

There is a large rock and flash of blood. A bright lantern is to one side. Shiny, crinkled objects are strewn on the ground. I hear a strange crack. There's a fence behind the trees, and I watch the dead man being slowly dragged toward it. There's a cavern beyond the fence. The lantern's gone dark. Now I hear angry words I can't understand. I run. And scream.

But who was this man? Who is his killer? Our family hasn't traveled much except for the one trip to Niagara Falls and another to Myrtle Beach with our neighbors where I can't ever recall ever being alone.

That would leave the crime happening on my own block, right under our noses. But I don't recall anyone suddenly disappearing around here; in Barton that would be historic news.

I look over my partially finished collage and the figure I had unexpectedly decided to place under a tree. It's a man, slightly hunched over and wearing a plaid hat, looking at the small ravine a short distance off. I don't usually place figures in my collages, and don't know why I did, but I'm going with it.

It's five o'clock Halloween night. Tyler and Ethan, already dressed in their pirate costumes, wait to haul in their monumental stash of candy with my mother trailing behind them at a safe distance. I'll be handing out the candy at our house since my dad isn't home.

I'm lighting our two jack-o-lanterns we have on the stoop when Gerald Zabinski walks towards our house with two large bags of candy bars. He waves from the sidewalk.

"I brought you and your brother some candy."

"Thank you." I take the bags from him.

"We usually hand it out to the kids in the neighborhood, but I thought I'd just give it to you two this year."

"You didn't have to do that, Mr. Zabinski." Now I feel kind of sorry for him because I think this has something to do with Sheba and his brother August.

"Your cat doing okay?"

"Yeah." I don't tell him about her stitches and ten-day quarantine.

"August just gets a little carried away sometimes. He never means harm. In fact, he really likes your cat."

"He does?"

"Yeah. He was petting it today, in fact."

"He was?"

"Yes."

Gerald Zabinski is lying. Sheba hasn't been out of the house in over a week. The candy's one thing but to make up a story about Sheba and August to make his brother look good is another.

"Well, Happy Halloween to you." He goes back down the walk.

I hurry inside and shut the door. I watch him through our front window. It's not until I see him in the shadows that it occurs to me he's wearing what he always wears—a plaid hat.

Mr. Silva commends the class on our *Hamlet* essays, singling out Cole's as "exceptionally perceptive and relevant". He asks Cole to read the short piece to the class. Cole chose the passage where Polonius advises his son:

This above all: To thine own self be true,
And it must follow, as the night the day,
Thou canst not then be false to any man.

Cole, in his usual unassuming manner, suggests that what seems to be virtuous wisdom and a guide for daily living is actually Polonius telling his son to project a good image and take care of Number One before doing anything for anybody else. Cole draws a parallel with today's big business and corporations bent on convincing people they're only thinking of others as they gouge you for money. Mr. Silva tells Cole he's awfully young to be a cynic.

Hannah and I pass in the hall, but she looks the other way. I notice Victoria has been eating lunch at another table. Still, Victoria is not particularly friendly towards me, so I keep my distance with her.

Deep down I'm not totally convinced things are over with Hannah and me, but it no longer has the hold it once did. Maybe since I figured out I'm not a murderer after all.

When I get home from school today I take Sheba out into our backyard. It's day eight of her sentence, but I figure it's close enough to let her out with supervision. I lean against our garage and watch her sniff the grass and bushes. Suddenly she runs from me and starts to climb between the slats of our rail fence over to Zabinskis' yard. I rush to stop her. I manage to grab her before she slips through. I'm on my knees with her in my arms and about to stand up when I see a mound of large rocks, a pile at least three feet high and just as wide in the brothers' backyard. The rocks are stacked up behind a thick patch of trees deep in their spacious back area. I stare at this sight and try to imagine what the rocks are doing there.

Then, without warning, Sheba leaps out of my arms and catapults over the fence. I call to her, but she ignores me and continues on. I jump the fence after her and follow her to behind the trees.

I stand staring at this part of Zabinskis' yard which I've never seen before. I freeze at the sight: trees, patches of dirt, rocks. So many rocks. I move to the wire fence, which frames the back part of their yard and overlooks the ravine on the other side. I can hear the water running through the large, sunken pipe in the adjacent culvert.

As I take in what's before me, my stomach drops. An eerie feeling floods me, and I sense the familiar pounding in my chest. It's all here in front of me. All but a dead man with one shoe. Everything fits.

I want to get home, fast, but I can't find Sheba anywhere. I can't stay here looking for her. I need to get back to Tyler. Nothing feels safe. As I turn to go, the first thing I see are the white Nike shoes and long, tattered winter coat. It's August Zabinski.

"Whatcha doing there?"

"My cat jumped the fence. I was trying to find her." I take several steps away from him.

"She's not here," he says.

"Okay, I'm sorry to bother you."

I leap over the fence and run across our yard as fast as I can move toward our house. I trip on the steps and hit my knee before reaching the porch. I'm out of breath as I slam the door shut. I stand in the kitchen barely able to breath.

Tyler comes in and asks me what's wrong. I tell him Sheba's in August Zabinski's yard.

"Mom said she couldn't go out for two more days! She's gonna be mad."

I need to try and get Sheba back without alarming Tyler. If August hurt Sheba once, he'll do it again.

I go to the back door and call her name while Tyler opens a can of tuna to help lure Sheba out of hiding. He heads outside before I can stop him.

Suddenly the front door flies open and my mother comes in carrying the cat. "What was Sheba doing outside?!" my mother snaps.

"She's back!" I run to the door. I'm even glad to see my mother. "I took her out for some air and she escaped."

"Could we please keep her inside until she gets her stitches out? Is that too much to ask?"

"I've got to talk to you, Mom."

"Can it wait till after supper?"

"No, it can't."

"All right." We go into the kitchen. I close the door behind us.

"It's the Zabinskis."

"What about them?"

"They're dangerous. August is anyway. Maybe both of them."

"What are you talking about? You mean because of what happened with Sheba?"

"No. Well, that, too, but because of what I saw there today."

"My God, what happened?" There's a rise of panic in her voice.

"Nothing today, but it's what I saw in their yard when I went to get Sheba."

At first I struggle with how to begin, but then decide to start with the details of my dreams and how I now know that they're memories of something I witnessed. I tell her about the strange rock pile there, the incline, the dirt path.

She listens carefully as I speak and at one point even reaches over and squeezes my hand. I feel enormous relief to tell what I've been holding in for so long. My mother's support is the anchor I've needed all along. I should've done it sooner.

"Oh, Helen," she says. "How awful. I knew your dreams were bad, but this. How terrible for you, sweetheart."

"It's horrible, all of it, Mom."

"But what does this have to do with the Zabinskis?"

"What do you mean what does this have to do with the Zabinskis? Everything! The rock that killed the man. The murder. It all fits, everything. The trees, the rocks, especially the rocks. And the ravine. The culvert. That's the hollow opening."

"Are you telling me you think one of those men killed somebody?"

"Yes."

"Right there in their backyard?"

"Yes. And I think maybe it was their nephew who used to live there."

"Orin?"

"Yes. He suddenly moves to Canada one day. Isn't that weird?"

"You think they killed their nephew Orin and you saw it happen?"

"Maybe. Yeah. I'm not sure."

My mother looks at me. Tears well up in her eyes. I rarely see my mother cry, so I'm not sure what to make of this.

"This is my fault," she says, tears flowing now. She grabs a napkin. "I should have made you go to a real therapist."

"Therapist?"

"Yes. I let you talk me out of it. I let you go to your guidance counselor instead. I knew that wasn't enough."

"Did you hear anything I just said?"

"Yes, I did. And what I heard was very, very upsetting."

"What's upsetting? That the crazy man next door killed somebody and I probably saw it happen?"

"No, that you think that's what happened and that you think you witnessed it. That's what's so disturbing, Helen."

"Oh, my God, you don't believe me."

"Do you know how this all sounds, Helen? Do you hear yourself?"

"I know what I saw and what I keep seeing in my dreams."

"Your dreams, yes. Dreams are not reality."

"These are different. That's what I'm trying to tell you."

"You need help, honey."

"I saw something! Why don't you believe me?" I'm shouting now.

"Did you see a man getting bludgeoned to death out there today?" My mother whispers for Tyler's benefit.

"No."

"Or a body dragged away?"

"No, but the setting's the same."

"Did you see any of that today?"

"No, because it didn't happen today. I'm talking about the yard. It's where I think it happened and where I saw it a long time ago."

"Trees, rocks, dirt. Helen, for God's sake, that stuff's everywhere."

"What about the huge pile of rocks back there? What's that for?"

"I don't know, but they're just rocks."

"Just rocks." I repeat my mother's words.

"Yes. It's not a crime to have a rock pile in your back yard."

A sudden calm suddenly washes over me. I know defeat when it's staring me in the face. I should have known that she–and soon my father–would never believe me about any of it. It was stupid to think so. I get up to leave the kitchen.

"Helen, sit down."

"No, it's okay. You're right, it's just rocks and trees."

"You're just letting your imagination get the best of you, honey."

"I probably am."

"I want to be supportive, sweetheart, but you have to step back and see how this all sounds."

"I know."

"Really?"

"Yeah."

"Do you see where I'm coming from with this?"

"Uh-huh."

"You do, really?"

"It doesn't matter."

"It does matter. *You* matter, Helen."

"Do I?"

"Yes! Why would you say that? What do you mean?"

"Nothing. I'm tired. I'm going to go to bed."

"You haven't eaten."

"I'm not hungry."

"Helen, please. Sit down and let's talk."

I'm almost out the kitchen door. I turn back to my mother. "Maybe Sheba should stay inside from now on, be an indoor cat."

I'd like to tell my parents they should keep Tyler inside, too. But there's no point. That would be the advice of a crazy girl.

CHAPTER FIFTEEN

My mother wasted no time setting up an appointment with a shrink. The good news is the psychologist can't fit me in for a month. Patient overload. Says something about the residents of Barton.

I tell Cole about my discovery in the Zabinski backyard and my theory that it might be their nephew Orin who they killed. Cole's not only fascinated by the apparent link but asks if he can look around himself. I'd be happy to have him survey the area, but between August and my parents, it could be a tricky proposition.

Cole walks me home today. We discuss various angles to the case, as we now call it. I keep referring to August as the murderer when Cole brings up a point. "Maybe August isn't the killer."

"Then who?"

"His brother?"

"I don't think Gerald would kill anybody. August is the most likely. We know he hurt Sheba. And you've met him."

"That doesn't automatically make him a killer. I'm just saying. Sometimes it's the person you don't suspect."

"I just assumed Gerald helped August cover up the deed so they didn't take August away. He protects him all the time."

"You said there were two people in your dreams."

"Yeah, the killer and the dead guy. I think there were two. It's kind of murky, as you know."

"But if both brothers were involved, that would make three."

"You're right."

Just then I recall the sketch of my second collage where I've included figures in my drawing. I placed a man in the background and the figure of a man in a plaid hat.

"I guess it doesn't matter how many there were, just who did it, if the Zabinskis are the ones. I know it's not for sure, but things are adding up."

"It's easy to check out the nephew. I'll do that tonight. If it wasn't him, then who else do you think they might have killed?"

"I have no idea. Probably no one any of us knows."

"You think the body might be buried under the rocks?"

"Maybe, although that part doesn't fit with my dreams. I think the dead man was put in a tunnel or cave. Or a culvert. That's now what I think anyway."

Cole shakes his head. "A body would've been discovered in a city culvert. It's been years. There's no way. Same with the rock pile."

"Then in the ground, under the rocks maybe. Oh, I don't know. I don't know what to do."

"You don't have to do anything. Just let things happen the way they're gonna. The truth has a way of coming out."

Since going to my mother with my theory about the Zabinski brothers, she walks around like I've been diagnosed with a terminal illness. She tells Tyler not to bug me and actually asks if she can get me anything from the kitchen while I'm doing homework. She's arrives home earlier and earlier from work, probably in case I get any ideas about harming Tyler. She must think I've snapped, and, like we do with August, treads carefully as not to upset me.

The first few days my mother did this, it not only annoyed me, but depressed me as well. No one wants to be thought of as batty, but because I know I'm not, I decide to cash in on my mom's new approach. I tell her some chips and salsa would be nice while I work on math, then yell down for her to throw in a Gatorade while she's at it.

My father says he's concerned about the nightmares but is only mildly appalled at my murder theory. He tells my mother I've always been creative, and maybe she should try celebrating my eccentricities rather than damning them. My mother tells him if he was around more he might have a different perspective on things.

It's interesting that neither of my parents will even consider the possibility that the men next door could be culpable in some crime, or that what I see in my dreams could be real. My mother saw what August did to Sheba, but somehow she's written that off as a minor nuisance.

I've been dreaming almost every night and recording them when I wake up, but they're mostly blurred thoughts that don't tell me anything new. Grandma Wren was in my dream last night, though. She sat on a lawn chair, reading. I said hello, but she just looked up and smiled. The smile is new.

A certain level of peace has come over me since my discovery next door. Not that August isn't still creepy, although I haven't even seen him since that afternoon, but it's taken much of my fear away. It doesn't remove whatever I witnessed, but I now have what I believe is a reference point for the dreams and memories.

And as far as the rest of it, well, Cole's right, it's better to just let things happen.

Tia's birthday is Thursday. I wove her a fabric bracelet out of white muslin, then dipped and blocked it in different shades of India ink to represent Think Ink. I hope she gets the connection.

I haven't talked or seen my cousin since telling her my parents couldn't help her, but I'm stopping at her place after school today since I can't go Thursday. I haven't decided whether to tell her about the Zabinski brothers or not.

There's a chance Hannah could be in the coffee house, but I want a chai and I'm not letting fear of running into her stop me. I also want to look at the *Nobody Knows...* board. My guess is Cole's been checking it for me, although he hasn't directly said so.

While waiting for my tea I glance around the booths and tables, but don't see anyone I know. I walk over to the postings and in spite of myself I feel my heart start to pound at what I might find. I read each note carefully and once again am struck by the thoughts and struggles of everyday people. *Nobody Knows... I still think I'm fat. Nobody Knows. I haven't seen my dad in two years. Nobody Knows... I'm in love with Jacob.* I scan farther down to another post and recognize the handwriting immediately. *Nobody Knows... Helen Wren is freaking awesome.* Cole. He's been in here all right.

The first thing that hits me as I walk into Think Ink is the smell of cigarette smoke. Tia doesn't let people smoke in her place, so that leaves only one person who would ignore her wishes and light up.

My aunt comes rushing past me with a brick as I'm about to close the door. "Hold on, Helen," she says without saying hi or looking at me. She pushes the door back open and wedges the brick to prop open the door.

"I've got to air this place out before Tia gets back." She waves her arms around to clear the smoke. "Okay," she says loudly, walking around, still waving her arms. "So I had one lousy cigarette in here, big deal. Oh, no, not second-hand smoke! Oh, no!" She's mocking Tia now.

Carol's hair seems to have reached new heights, something I didn't think possible. The blond streaks sit varnished and startled among the dark arrangement about her head. There's a can of beer on the counter. She's wearing red ankle boots and a pair of jeans I swear are Tia's. Or were Tia's. They may be stretched beyond repair and never fit my cousin again.

"Tia met a friend for lunch and isn't back yet. Some lunch. It's going on three hours. Business is slow right now. I thought I'd clean the place up for her while she's out."

"I'll wait awhile if that's okay. I have a birthday present for her."

"How nice." She forces a fake smile. "Have a seat." She takes a long swig of beer and straightens the magazines on the table.

"I'll have to give your mom a call about Thanksgiving."

"Okay." I don't know what she means, but this can't be good.

"Your mother called and invited us over for Thanksgiving dinner," she says, as if reading my mind. "I thought I'd bring my sweet potato dish. Everybody loves it."

What could my mother have been thinking? Guilt, that's what.

"I was surprised when your mother called since you usually go to her parents' house for the holiday."

"They're going to Florida this year, to see my uncle."

"Must be nice to be able to just pick up and fly south whenever you want." She takes another swig of beer. "But, dinner will be nice, even if we are second choice."

If Tia doesn't come back soon, I'm leaving. Five minutes with Carol is my limit. The phone rings and Carol answers it with such ease and command that I wonder if she's taken over the front desk.

As Carol hangs up the phone, she throws back the last of her beer, then crushes the can on the counter. She aims for the waste basket a short distance away, but the can misses and hits the floor.

"Are you getting cold?" she asks.

"Kind of." Actually, it's freezing.

"I could shut the door. I think it's okay in here now."

Just then Tia walks in. "Ma! I asked you not to smoke in here," she says, putting her bag down. She doesn't see me.

"What are you talking about?" Carol's standing near the doorway. Even the wind doesn't move her hair.

"The cigarette smell. Plus, it's like thirty degrees in here now."

Carol removes the brick. "I was just airing out the place."

"You were smoking and you opened the door to get rid of it."

I get up from my chair. "Hi, Tia."

"Melon, hi." She seems glad to see me.

"Three-hour lunch on a work day, must be nice." Carol picks up her beer can from the floor and puts it in the trash.

Tia spins around and glares at her mother. "Did anybody come in while I was gone?" she asks in a defensive tone.

"No."

"Then it doesn't really matter how long my lunch was, does it?"

"I suppose not." Carol adjusts a plastic curl behind her ear. "But watch your tone with me, missy."

"Were you waiting long, Melon?" Tia is ignoring her mother.

"No, I just got here. I brought you something for your birthday." I hand her the gift.

"That's so sweet." She opens the box and takes out the bracelet. "Oh, my God, I love it. You did it in inks, it's perfect!"

Of course Tia would get the ink theme. My aunt doesn't comment on the gift.

"Don't forget, I want to see your new collage when you're done, too."

"I had to start over. Sheba got hurt and bled on it."

"One more reason not to own a cat," says Carol, as if bleeding cats are a common occurrence. "I hate cats. They're sneaky and devious."

"But they're not," I say.

"Dogs are the best pet."

"Then why didn't you let Bass and me ever have one?" Tia's trying on the bracelet.

"What are you talking about? I suggested getting a dog once and you kids said no way. You made such a fuss I dropped the idea."

"Bass totally begged you for a dog. We both did."

"No, you didn't."

"Yes, we did. In fact, you told Bass he could have one for his birthday one year, then you gave him a soccer ball. He didn't even play soccer."

"I gave you kids whatever you wanted. Anything you wanted, anything, if I could possibly afford it." Carol looks like she's about to cry and I realize she's getting drunk. "Do you know how much I sacrificed for you and Bass?"

"Yeah, okay, Ma."

"I did whatever it took to protect you kids, to make you happy. I made sure you kids had whatever you wanted. Even after your father walked out on us."

"He didn't walk out on us. You kicked him out."

"He moved across country, didn't he?"

"Yeah."

"Found himself a new lady."

"So? You date—or used to, anyway."

"But I had to take care of you kids."

"Gee, sorry," Tia smirks.

Carol takes out a cigarette and heads for the front door. She grabs a can of beer from the small frig on her way out.

"This is what I live with now," Tia whispers. "I'm twenty-three, but I feel like I'm forty-three. Look at the bags under my eyes. How awful are they?"

"You look great, Tia." She doesn't.

"She's got to get a job and get out of my place."

"Maybe my dad can find her something at the main office." I heard the words as they came out of my mouth.

"That would be great!"

"I can't promise anything, but I'll ask."

"Thank you!"

I get up to leave. "Well, I'd better get home."

"I'll walk out with you." Tia grabs her jacket. "I get away from her any chance I can now," says Tia, walking. "Lately she's been obsessing on how she took care of Bass and me. And believe me, we did not get everything we wanted. Just ask my brother."

"About the dog?"

"The dog, a bike, the zoo. She never took us anywhere. Grandma and Grandpa Wren gave us stuff, but not my mother. She gave Bass almost nothing. She was a lot nicer to me. It's like she hated men, even her own son."

"But she dated, you said."

"Except nobody stuck around. There was one guy she went out with for a long time I really liked. Bass loved him. But, of course, my mother ruined that, too. He went camping with us and everything, but then he split."

"The camping trip to Blackfoot Springs?"

"Yeah. Hey, that's right, you were with us, Melon. You were just little."

"Did you ever see him again?"

"Briefly. Or, my mom did, I guess. She returned his stuff that was at our house. He told her the real reason he left is he just couldn't handle having an instant family. So, there you go, it was mine and Bass's fault."

We're standing in front of the coffee shop. "Happy birthday, Tia."

"Thanks. Hey, Melon, how are you doing? I didn't even ask you. You know, with all the stuff you've been going through?"

"Better."

"Good, I'm glad." She doesn't ask more and I don't offer.

Since my dad's home and my mom switched her hours at work, we're having one of those rare, weekday family meals together tonight. Continuing with the let's-try-to-keep-Helen-happy mode, my mother makes my favorite meal—curried rice with vegetables. I'm starting to enjoy this.

"Aunt Carol was at Tia's shop today." I open with casual news and figure I'll work up to asking my dad if he can find her a job.

"And how is Carol?" My mother can barely hide her contempt.

"She's driving Tia crazy."

"No surprise there."

"She was talking about how hard it was taking care of Tia and Bass without a husband."

"It was very tough for Carol after the divorce," my father says with an unexpected burst of compassion.

"Well, she should've snagged one of the men who came around then," says my mother. "There were enough of them."

"I thought she was going to marry the one guy," says my dad. "He was real good to her and the kids. Super nice fella."

"At first he was," says my mother, "but he turned out not to be, remember? He told Carol he got cold feet about being a family man."

"That's right."

"What was his name again?" asks my father.

"Barry."

"Oh, yeah, Barry."

CHAPTER SIXTEEN

I am running when suddenly someone grabs me and picks me up. I'm flung into an enclosed space, and a cover is thrown over me. Grandma Wren is there. She tells me I just awoke from a bad dream and that everything is all right. I'm confused why she's saying that. It wasn't a dream. I was just outside, running. I'm still out of breath and my knee hurts where I fell. I smell burnt marshmallows and damp ashes from a fire.

I sit up and look at the clock on my nightstand. Two o'clock. Am I awake? I can't even tell, but I recall what I just saw.

It's been a long night, and I'm surprised I fell asleep at all, if I even did. Who knows? When my mother said the word Barry tonight, I was chilled to the bone. It's the same word I've been crying out all these months. Is it possible? It seems unlikely given who the guy was. This Barry dated Carol, dumped Carol and moved on. End of story.

Yet something leaves me unsettled.

I lean back on the pillow and close my eyes. *It's up to you now, Helen.* My grandmother's words rise up again. I turn on the light and grab my notebook. I write. More time passes as I drift in and out of sleep, till finally morning light streams through the blinds. The notebook has fallen and slipped to the floor. I pick it up and read what I've written, then page back over the past entries. I pore over each one carefully to assure that what I suspect is there. It is.

Yes, my grandmother's been trying to reach me. She's been coming to me in my dreams because she, too, knows of the horror I witnessed long ago.

She knows because she was there.

CHAPTER SEVENTEEN

Cole and I are huddled over our coffee mugs. I had texted him earlier to meet me right after school.

"I'm sure my grandmother saw the murder, too. Or at least something," I tell him. "She told me I was just dreaming, but I wasn't."

"She told you in a dream you were just dreaming in a dream?"

"You make it sound so complicated."

"It is, I guess."

"I think she wanted me to believe I didn't really see anything when I saw the murder, so she told me it was just a bad dream."

"Why do you think that?"

"It's what I saw, plus I went over all my journal notes. It just fits."

"That's not really much to go on."

"It's all I've got. Don't bail on me now, Cole. You're the only one I can talk to about this."

"I would never bail on you! I'm just not sure where this is going. How was she there? Was she with you at your house when you saw the guys next door?" He slurps the foam off his caramel macchiato.

"Maybe, yet if she saw August Zabinski kill someone, she would've called the police, not silenced me."

"Unless she was covering up for the guy."

"Why would she do that?"

"Maybe they had a thing going."

"Eeew. I don't even think they ever met. Eeew."

"Then how does she figure into all this?"

"I don't know."

"I checked Orin Zabinski in Canada. There's no Orin Zabinski anywhere that I can find."

"I knew it!"

And I also checked missing persons in the Barton area for the last twelve years on my dad's police website."

"And?"

"Nothing that fits."

"Then this points back to Orin. But I still don't know how my grandmother fits into this scenario."

"Maybe your grandmother's not one of the players."

"She is. I'm positive."

"You were positive you killed somebody, too, and you didn't."

"This is different."

Cole shakes his head. "I know you feel sure about your grandmother, but there's more to go on with these guys. A grisly stoning like you described wouldn't have taken place in a public area. That narrows the choices."

"I know, but I just can't shake off this thing with Grandma Wren. It's too real."

"Did you stay at your grandmother's house when you were younger? Maybe you saw something over there in her neighborhood."

"I thought of that, but she lived in an apartment building, hardly any trees. None of the scenery fits."

"Then it doesn't add up that your grandmother and the Zabinskis were together at the crime scene."

"I know."

"Then this is what we've got: your grandmother, you, the perp and the victim. Outside."

"And a tent."

"A tent? You never mentioned a tent."

"In last night's dream. I think she grabbed me and threw me in a tent."

"Like a camping tent?"

"Yeah, maybe."

"So, you're saying you went camping with your grandmother?"

"No, that's just it. I only camped once with my aunt and cousins."

"Cousins from this same grandmother's side?"

"Yeah."

We look at each other.

I think for a moment. "Barry."

"What?"

"A guy named Barry was camping with us, too. I yell out some version of that name in my sleep."

"You're just telling me this now?"

"It might be a coincidence."

"And I might be the pope."

I jump up. "Come on, we're going to see my cousin."

We head the few doors down to Think Ink. Tia's standing talking with a customer when we walk in. I look around and am relieved not to see my aunt anywhere. Tia looks at Cole, then back at me and smiles.

I introduce Cole to Tia and because she's just about to take her customer in the back room, I rush to my question.

"Tia, remember the camping trip we were just talking about yesterday?"

"Uh-huh."

"Grandma Wren didn't go, did she?"

"No. Why?"

"Nothing. I was just telling Cole about her and was thinking about stuff when I was younger, that's all."

Cole and I make a hasty exit, leaving Tia to her client.

"Well, strike two," I say on our way back to my house.

As we turn onto my street, I see a small gathering of people in front of the Zabinski house. As we get closer I see Gerald and August Zabinski, my mother, and a man I don't recognize standing near the curb. There are two large suitcases on the sidewalk and a van with the engine running in their driveway.

There's no way to avoid them, so I say hello.

"Helen, come here." My mother takes my arm and walks me up to the man I don't know. "This is Orin Zabinski, August and Gerald's nephew from Canada. I don't know if you remember him, but he used to live next door, too."

"Hello, Helen," Orin says. "You've sure grown up since I saw you last. You were just a little thing when I left."

"Hello," I say, barely able to get the words out. I'm staring at the living dead. I'm looking at the man I thought was skeletal remains beneath the rock pile next door, the man I was almost sure August bludgeoned to death.

"Orin moved to Canada," my mother says.

"Yep, just home for a visit." Orin looks a little like Gerald but a much cleaner version.

I don't dare turn and look at Cole, but he's got to be having the same reaction: strike three.

"August is going away for a while," my mother tells me. "Let's wish him well."

"Good-bye," I say and turn to go.

Orin helps August into the van and shuts the door."

"Poor guy," says my mother.

Cole and I are tripping over each other to talk. He goes first. "This doesn't mean it didn't happen over there. It's just means it wasn't the nephew."

"This changes things now."

Suddenly a text comes in on my cell. I look at my phone. It's from Tia.

> idk how I cld forget. grandma was camping 2.she almost set tent on fire. speaking of flames ur boy is sizzzling hot!

I close my phone and look at Cole. "Oh, yeah, things have changed all right."

Before I even try to absorb Tia's info, I go to my mother to see if she can verify that my grandmother was on the camping trip. Tia may have gotten it wrong, although I doubt it, given she remembers a fire.

"Yes," my mother says. "The only way I was going to go to Boston was if your grandmother was there to help Aunt Carol with you, being so little and all."

It's interesting how a few words can define a moment, how a benign comment from one person can illuminate and change another. My grandmother was there and what I thought was a tent in my dreams was very likely a tent. And a man named Barry was there also, a name I've been repeating in the dark for months, maybe even years.

There's only one time and one place this incident—this dream, this nightmare—could have happened. Blackfoot Springs, twelve years ago. Blackfoot Springs, with its rocks and crevices, its caves and tunnels, its winding stream and its remote campsites, tucked among the hills and backwoods of southern Ohio.

CHAPTER EIGHTEEN

Hamlet had his issues—ask anyone—yet I have been rooting for the guy since page one. But now that we've finished the play, I'm starting to rethink things. Hamlet really wasn't all that nice, plus he justified pretty much everything he did, including a couple of murders, all to just end up dead himself. Talk about no winners.

Call us a couple of geeks, but Cole and I watched the movie version of *Hamlet* together before the exam. I asked him if he would because, although I wanted to see the film, the last act is so full of death and bodies that I was afraid it would unnerve me watching it alone. At least that's what I told myself.

Sitting in my family room with the credits still rolling, Cole and I continue where we left off, lowering our voices in case anyone hears.

"Assuming everything happened at the camp ground, it would seem this Barry guy either killed someone or was killed," says Cole, picking the last kernels of popcorn out of the bowl.

"Except Barry can't be the victim because he didn't die. Tia said he showed up later."

"Then Barry could be the killer."
"Yes."
"Who'd he kill?"
"And why."
"There's no body, no missing person. Nothing to go on."
"Yet," I say, walking him to the door.

Since placing the murder at Blackfoot Springs, my dreams have stopped. Just when I'd like to have more information, my unconscious fails me.

Tia and I arranged to meet this week for her to look at my summer solstice collage. I really just want to pick her brain as subtly as I can about Barry and the camping trip.

There's a knock on my bedroom door. It's my mother.

"Got a minute?"
"Yeah."

She walks in and sits down. "We never talked about the fact that Orin showed up next door."

"I know."
"How do you feel about that?"
"Kinda stupid." (And very disappointed.)

"You shouldn't feel stupid, but I hope you're at least relieved. This is what I meant about making up stories without facts."

"Yeah, but I told you I dropped all that stuff anyway. I know now it was all just in my head." I tell her exactly what she wants to hear.

"Good, Helen. That's good!"
"Do I still have to go to the therapist?"
"Yes."
"Why?"
"Because."
"Because you think I'm bonkers."
"I don't think that, Helen."
"You think I'm something."
"Nosy, maybe," she says with a laugh.
"Nosy?"
"I'm just quoting Aunt Carol." She gets up to leave. "I was talking to her today about plans for Thanksgiving and she said you're very nosy, asking Tia about when you were little."

"So? What's wrong with that?"

"Nothing. But you know Carol, it doesn't take much to set her off."

"Apparently."

The plan was to meet Tia at the coffee shop, but she texts me on my way over and asks me to come to Think Ink instead.

Carol's standing by the door as I approach. She holds it open for me as I walk in. "Well, if it isn't the family brain here to pay a visit." She flashes a broad smile. "Come on in. Tia won't be long."

There's something different about my aunt, but I can't put my finger on it. She's not wearing Tia's jeans this time, and her hair is tamer than usual, but I don't think that's it.

"How are you, Helen? School good?"

"Yeah, fine."

"That's great. I know what a good student you are. Honors classes, senior art."

I look up, surprised she knows any of this about me.

"Oh, I keep up with what's going on," she continues. "You probably don't think so, but I do. What are aunts for if they don't know what their nieces and nephews are up to?"

At first I think she's drunk, but then I realize it's just the opposite: She's sober. That's what's different. She's usually at some level of inebriation, but today she appears to be at zero.

"But I'm not the nosy one around here, am I?" She smiles her fake smile.

"Whatever."

I weigh the decision whether to pursue any of my theory with my aunt. She is, after all, indirectly involved in my theory. It may have been her boyfriend who killed someone. And Grandma Wren is her mother. Who better to fill me in than Carol? Yet if my encounter backfires, the story will go straight to my parents. It may anyway. I choose my words very carefully, hoping to extract the necessary information, but only disclose what I absolutely have to.

"I've been having a lot of dreams about Grandma Wren."

"You mentioned that once before. The yellow sweater."

"Yeah. Well, I know this is going to sound crazy, but it's like she's trying to tell me something."

"Oh, you mean she talks to you." There's a hint of sarcasm in her voice. "What do you think she's trying to tell you?"

"Umm, something."

"Like what?"

I pause, not sure whether to continue.

"Like what? Speak."

"I think we saw something bad happen."

"Who?"

"Grandma and me."

"When?"

"Well, that's just it. I think maybe at Blackfoot Springs a long time ago. That's why I was asking about it."

"You couldn't possibly remember that trip. You were so young. I barely remember it."

"I know, but I have dreams about it."

"What could you have seen on a camping trip that was so bad? A bear? A snake?"

"No, nothing like that."

"Then what?"

I pause. "A murder. A horrible, bloody, murder."

"What?!"

"Yes."

"How awful, Helen. What makes you think you saw an actual murder of all things?"

"Dreams, weird memories."

"Oh, your dreams indeed."

"I believe it happened, and I think Grandma thought so, too."

"Sounds pretty out there to me."

"I know how it sounds."

"You're upset about something a dead person supposedly told you in a dream."

"It's not just from Grandma. There's been other stuff."

"Well, to say your story's a stretch is an understatement. My, my, you really are a handful, aren't you?"

Her condescending attitude is very annoying, but I press on. "I think it might have had something to do with your boyfriend, Barry, who went camping with us."

"Barry? Gee, I haven't thought of him in years. But you can't possibly remember Barry."

"I've been calling out the name Barry in my sleep."

"That doesn't mean it's my old Barry."

"I don't know anybody else named Barry."

"You don't know this Barry, either! Really, Helen."

I already regret talking to her.

"I thought you could help about Barry, but just never mind. It doesn't matter."

"Oh, go ahead then, just spit it out, will you?" she asks with sudden impatience. "What? What?!"

"Okay. I think he might have killed someone," I blurt out.

"Who, Barry?!!"

"I know it sounds crazy."

"You honestly think the Barry I once knew killed somebody on a camping trip while you and my mother watched."

"Yeah." The dripping mockery in her voice makes me cringe.

She walks over to the frig and grabs a beer.

"Where were the rest of us while this was happening?" she continues with her caustic tone. "My kids weren't there with you?"

"I just know what I see in my dreams."

"That's quite a story."

"I know."

"You just made a very serious accusation, missy."

"I just said I think... maybe."

"Have you told anyone else this?"

"No." I don't mention Cole.

"I wouldn't go around telling people this."

"I don't."

"Do your parents know?"

"No! And I would appreciate it if you didn't tell them either. I only told you because of Barry."

Carol leans back on the sofa and opens her can of beer. "Well, I'll tell you one thing," she says. "Barry was not that great of a guy. He treated me like crap, my kids like crap, even my mother, and nobody liked him. Still, there's no way Barry would kill anybody. My God, Helen, how crazy this whole discussion is. Really, you need to get another hobby."

I'm thinking what a different view Tia and my parents had of Barry.

She suddenly starts to laugh. "I'd love to see Barry's face if he heard your story. I feel like looking him up just to tell him."

"Please don't." I get up and start for the door.

"Oh, sit down. I'm just having a little fun with you."

"All I know is Grandma's trying to tell me something."

"Tell her I said hi next time you see her."

"Make fun of me all you want. I believe something happened at Blackfoot Springs."

"You probably saw some kids wrestling or something. Quit torturing yourself, Helen."

"I'm going to figure this out."

"Good luck then."

Tia comes in carrying a bag of groceries. As glad as I am to see her and be released from the jaws of my aunt, I now have no desire to show Tia my collage. Carol has ruined the mood. I was a fool to think I could trust her.

"I have to go," I tell Tia.

Carol walks past us and heads outside for a cigarette.

"Wait, let me see your collage first."

"That's okay, another time. I gotta go."

"Okay, then," says Tia. "Nice to see ya."

I walk out the front door. "Bye," I force myself to say to my aunt as I pass by her.

"Bye, Helen," she says through a cloud of smoke. "Just give those dreams a rest, will ya? Enough with the rock and blood and ghost stuff."

I continue on to the end of the street and when I'm certain I'm no longer in Carol's view, I stop, unable to go on. My legs are starting to give from under me.

I never once mentioned a rock to Carol.

CHAPTER NINETEEN

I'm still standing in a store doorway down from Think Ink. I start to text Cole but call instead, asking if he can meet me right away. He hears the panic in my voice and says he can be there in ten minutes on his bike. We agree to meet two blocks further than where I am. I now feel too close to Tia's shop to be comfortable.

By the time Cole arrives, I'm freezing. We go inside Wendy's down the street. He brings over two sodas and some fries. I fill him in on my conversation with Carol.

"She actually said a rock. I never once said anything about a rock."

"Are you positive?"

"Of course I am," I say, annoyed.

"Okay, yeah, sorry."

"The reason I'm so positive is because I intentionally didn't mention any specifics about the murder. I made a point of not doing that because I wanted to see if she brought up anything, any details on her own. And she did. I sure wasn't expecting this, though."

"But what does it mean? Carol saw Barry kill somebody, too?"

"Maybe."

He sits thinking. "Or—"

"Are you thinking what I am?"

"Carol's the one who did it."

"If she wasn't the witness, killer is the only other option. How else would she know about a rock?"

"Who would she have killed and why?" He dips a fry into some ketchup.

"I don't know how she could've pulled off a murder with others nearby."

"I don't think it was that nearby. In my dreams, it was more remote. Maybe I wandered off and my grandmother went after me."

"Do you remember when I said your grandmother might have tried to shut you up because she was protecting somebody?"

"Yeah."

"Wouldn't she have done that to protect her daughter?"

"Yes. But it still doesn't explain who Carol would've killed. I mean, she's not my favorite person, but I can't believe she would murder someone. It just isn't possible."

"We don't know for sure that Barry was alive after the camping trip. You said that your aunt was the only one who saw him after he abandoned them at the campsite."

I think back to Tia's conversation. "True. She said Aunt Carol went by herself to Barry's place to return his things."

Cole and I look at each other.

"I know what I've got to do now," I tell him.

"Text me as soon as you get his last name."

I didn't even have to explain to Cole the next step. He just knew.

My dad can remember scores from the last ten years of the World Series, but he's useless with people's names. I had hoped to avoid approaching my mother about Barry's last name, but since my father has no idea and my mother has a memory like a steel trap, I have no choice but to ask her. I'm reluctant to do so because I'm half expecting (and dreading) Carol will call about my confrontation with her at Tia's yesterday.

"Wilson, Williams," my mother's trying to recall. "Willet. That's it, Willet. Why do you want to know? You didn't even know him." This is why I wanted to avoid my mother. My father doesn't ask probing questions.

"You and Dad were just talking about him. I thought maybe I go to school with one of his kids."

She gives a small laugh. "What are you trying to do, fix Carol back up with him?" She returns to her laptop. "Anyway," she says, looking back at her screen, "he wasn't from around here. He lived west, closer to Toledo."

I immediately text the name and area to Cole, who texts back that he's out with his parents and can't do anything until tomorrow.

I finish my homework and go back to working on my collage. I keep looking at the figure that I've drawn, the one with the plaid cap, a cap much like the one Gerald Zabinski wears.

It's not until English class that I get a chance to talk to Cole. He tells me he'll do the research on the police website after school.

"My aunt still hasn't called my mother. I keep waiting. I know she will."

"Not if she's involved. The last thing she'd want to do is draw attention to the story."

"Or, she'll bring it up so I look totally wacko, which will make her look innocent."

Cole says he'll let me know as soon as he researches the police site later today.

Sheba hasn't been outdoors since the day she jumped the fence and I ran into August Zabinski. But since August is gone now—he's in a nursing home twenty miles from Barton—we're opening up her cat door. Even though it's safe, I go out into the backyard and follow her around while she sniffs and explores.

She apparently sees a mole or a bird and moves stealthily across the yard and toward the back. I follow her, curious to see what she's going to try to catch.

As she moves farther out, I glance over at the Zabinski yard and look at the rock pile. I move to the fence and lean on it, thinking how certain I was Orin Zabinski was either under those rocks or somewhere in that vast yard. Suddenly I look up and see Gerald Zabinski standing on the other side of the fence, face to face with me. He's so close I can smell his sour breath. I jump back. "You scared me," I tell him.

He just stares, silent. He's wearing the familiar plaid cap, plus now August's old, fur coat.

"Cold out here," he finally says.

"Yeah."

He continues to watch me as I pick up Sheba and run for the house.

"Where you going?" he asks.

Once inside I look back out and see he's moved up along the fence so he's now even with our back porch. He makes no attempt to move and continues to look at me through the window. I shut the blinds.

My mother's still at work, and I promised Tyler I'd play a game with him on the computer. It's hard to concentrate because I can't shake off the strange encounter I just had with Gerald.

Tyler's winning at Minecraft (of course) when Cole texts me.

Yes!! name, year, place.

I can hardly believe what I'm reading. Cole's clipped message couldn't be any clearer. Barry Willet went missing from Toledo twelve years ago. I can barely hold the phone. Tyler's yelling for me to take my turn. I quickly go through the motions when my mother walks in.

"Tyler, would you please go into the other room?" she asks without saying hello to either of us.

"We're right in the middle of a game!"

"Go! Now."

Tyler stomps off. My mother's clearly angry. I already know what it's about. She takes off her coat and throws it on a chair.

"Carol called me at work today."

"I figured she would."

"I don't know where to start. Telling her you think her boyfriend killed somebody. First the Zabinskis and now this! Truly, I don't know what to do with you. Is that why you were fishing for Barry's last name, to pursue some hallucination that you have?"

"Mom, listen to me. It's true. Barry Willet is missing, and I think Aunt Carol had something to do with it. It all fits. Everything."

"Like the story next door fit? Stop. Just stop, Helen."

"Aunt Carol mentioned a rock, and I never said anything about a rock. And she said Barry was a terrible person, but Tia and you and Dad said he was nice—"

"Enough! Not one more word!" She's pacing the floor, shouting.

Tyler bursts into the room, upset. "What's wrong, Mom?"

I go to my brother and hug him. "It's okay, Tyler. Mom and I are just having an argument, that's all. Everything's okay."

"No, everything is not okay," my mother says, pulling Tyler away from me. Now Tyler is crying.

"Go upstairs," she tells him. "Now." He runs up to his room.

"Mom, would you just listen to me?"

"No. I heard enough from Carol."

"You'll listen to her but not me." I run out of the room and start up the stairs.

She yells up after me. "And stay away from your brother."

The most painful part of this encounter is my mother's warning to stay away from Tyler. She believes I'm not only batty, but possibly dangerous, even to my own little brother.

Suddenly a text comes in. It's from Tia's shop cell.

Melon, can u come to TI now?
Big prob. It's bad. I need u.

The timing from Tia is perfect. I'm going to tell her everything. I'll call Cole on my way there, then I can offer further proof to Tia that Barry Willet never showed up again after the camping trip. Maybe it's even time to involve Cole's father in all this. I can't prove to Tia that her mother is a killer, but I can let her know Carol is far from honest and she knows more than she's telling.

Cole answers on the first ring. "It's true," he says, almost out of breath. "Barry Willet is registered missing. Twelve years ago, July. Last seen at his job in Toledo. And get this: they questioned your aunt and your grandmother at the time."

"Oh, my God, Cole. Listen, I'm on my way over to Tia's shop now. I'm telling her everything."

"I don't think you should do that. What if it backfires? She's more likely to take her mother's side than yours. And what if her mother's there?"

"She's not. Tia asked me to come. She wouldn't have asked if her mother was there. She needs to talk to me about something important."

"I don't like it. I'll go with you."

"It's okay. And it's also okay how chivalrous you're being. Very retro—but I like it. Oh, and Carol did call my mother. My mother doesn't believe me, of course."

"Be careful what you tell your cousin. Text me when you're done. Promise?"

"Promise."

I run down the stairs and go to the closet to grab my coat. My mother rushes into the foyer. "Where do you think you're going?"

"To Tia's shop."

"No, you're not. Stay away from there."

"Tia asked me to come and I'm going. And I'm telling her everything I told Aunt Carol and more. It's all true, Mom. I don't care if you believe me. I just know that Aunt Carol is involved in the disappearance of Barry Willet." I run out of the house without looking back, leaving the door open behind me.

The one mile to Tia's shop seems like five. I forgot a hat or gloves and the November air stings my face and hands.

When I arrive at Think Ink, there's no one in front. I call Tia's name, but there's no answer. I walk to the back room but don't see her anywhere. I walk back out to the front to wait when suddenly I hear someone come up behind me. I turn. It's Carol. I can tell by her demeanor that she's drunk.

"Nice of you to come, Helen."

"Where's Tia?"

"She stepped out."

"Will she be long?"

"I don't know. She didn't tell me where she was going." She's holding a beer.

"That's funny, because she asked me to come."

"That is funny, isn't it?"

"Yeah. It is."

Something's not right. Tia wouldn't just leave after asking me to rush over here. And if she did have to go, she would've texted me that. I look at my aunt. "Tia didn't tell me to come here, did she?"

"She blew out of here with no explanation."

"I'm gonna go."

"No, stay, this gives us a chance to talk."

"There's nothing to say."

"You accuse my friend of murder and there's nothing to say?"

"I accused him, you said I was wrong, so that's that. Can we just drop it?"

"Who else did you tell?"

"No one. There's nothing to tell. I don't have any proof of anything, so there would be no point."

"What if you had proof?" She moves in closer to me.

"Well, I don't know." She's starting to make me nervous. The woman has few boundaries when she's sober, let alone when she's drunk.

"You certainly don't. So why are you pursuing this?"

"For my own peace of mind."

"Isn't that sweet?" Her voice is full of sarcasm. She goes to the frig for more beer.

"I think I'd better go."

"Sit down." She's almost shouting now. I sit. "You're so sure of yourself, aren't you? But you don't know anything."

"Okay."

"Okay, what?"

"Okay, I don't know anything."

"I want to know how you really got interested in this story. And don't tell me it's because my dead mother talks to you."

"I told you, recurring dreams. Pictures in my head."

"Maybe your parents buy this dream stuff, but you and I both know you're getting your information some other way."

"I'm not. Don't believe me then."

She downs the rest of her beer and crushes the can. The sound of the can crushing gives me the chills. Suddenly I get a flash of the scene by the rocks that night. The shiny objects on the ground are flattened beer cans, strewn in the dirt. They're strewn around the man I now believe is Barry Willet and another person I've been unable to identify. Until now.

I stand up again. "I'm going." I make a rush for the exit, but Carol somehow gets ahead and blocks me. She locks the door.

"What's the hurry? Have a seat."

"I'm going home now."

"Tia will be here soon."

"I'll see her tomorrow."

"Sit and talk to me."

She begins to circle. Her words are becoming a little slurred. She goes to the frig. I grab my cell and quickly text Tia:

> I'm at TI. Ur mom is drunk
> and freaking me out

Carol comes back with a beer. She pulls out her cigarettes and lights up. "Want one?" She holds the pack up.

I shake my head. "Um, you know, Aunt Carol, you're right. This stuff I've been saying is really lame."

"Yeah?"

"Yeah. It's dumb."

"Where do you get your information from, Helen?"

"I told you, it's dumb."

"Who's talking to you?"

"Nobody."

"Just your dreams."

"Yes."

"You've become a real thorn in my side, ya know that?"

Suddenly a text comes in on my phone. It's from Tia:

> Why r u there? Why is my mom?
> We locked up together b4.

"I was right. Tia didn't text me, you did." I stare at my aunt.

"Aren't you the smart one." She grabs my cell and reads the text from Tia. She turns off the phone and puts it in her pocket.

"Please give me back my phone."

"Shut up."

"What do you want, Aunt Carol?"

"I want to know what you know and who you've told."

"Okay."

"The truth."

"In my dreams I saw a person from the back, a man—I don't know who it was—but I saw him get killed. That's all. And I haven't told anybody except you. But now you've told my parents, so that makes three who know."

"That's it? That's what's making you go around town like *CSI: Las Vegas*?"

"Yes."

"Nothing else?"

"No. What else would there be?" I leave out the part about the body being dragged. She hasn't, I noticed, asked how the person was killed. In fact, there are a lot of things she's not asking.

She gets up and comes over to me. "You're a little liar." She pulls me up by the collar. I scream. She gets in my face again. The smell of beer and cigarettes coming from her almost gags me. "If you mention this sick little story of yours to anyone, I'll make your life very, very miserable."

I push her hands away and break free as fast as I can, then run to Tia's work room to go out the back door, which leads to an alley. She runs after me, shouting.

"I've got the key to that door, too."

I try the door anyway, but it's locked. She runs ahead and stands in front of it.

"Let me out, now, Aunt Carol. I won't tell anybody anything. There's nothing to tell. It was just a wild story I made up because I was bored."

"You told Tia, didn't you?"

"No!"

"That's why she's been so unhappy lately."

"I didn't tell Tia."

She starts for me and I run back into the front area, trying the door which I know is futile. I bump into a vase on the counter and it smashes to the floor, shards of glass spraying everywhere.

"Please." I'm crying now. "Please just let me go. You're drunk and you don't know what you're doing."

"I am not drunk!" She reaches for me and I run into the back again, this time heading into the small bathroom. But as soon as I get in there and hook the flimsy latch, I realize it's useless because it's a short door and Carol can easily reach under or even climb under it if she wants to.

She is in a mad rage now, screaming obscenities at me as she rams her body into the thin door. I'm trying to step up onto the toilet seat when she reaches under and grabs one of my legs. She yanks so hard that I fall with a crash, my body slamming hard against the porcelain toilet frame as I go down. Pain seers up my spine and into my neck and I wonder for a moment if my back is broken.

Because I'm momentarily stunned, she's able to pull me out from under the stall with little trouble. Regaining some strength, I kick her as hard as I can. My boot heel catches her in the stomach. She lets out a cry. I kick her again. She kicks me in my side, although she's too drunk to aim very well. I struggle to my feet, planning to wrestle her for the phone so I can call 911.

For the first time I realize I could actually die, right now at the hands of this monster in front of me. I'm crying and moaning. I want to be home. I want my mother and father and my little brother. I want my bedroom. I want Sheba and all that's familiar. I want Cole. I don't want to die. I especially don't want to die like this.

The pain in my back soars as I lunge at my aunt. I reach for her pants pocket. She grabs my hair, and in one swift motion my neck is bent backward so I'm looking at the ceiling.

"Let go!" I scream. These are the first words uttered between us since she's attacked me. She pulls tighter on my hair, and I scream again. "Murderer!" Spit flies out of my mouth as I shout. "You killed Barry and everyone's going to know it. Everyone, including your kids, you killer!!"

Carol lets out a sound so primal it doesn't sound like it's coming from a human being.

Without any warning, her hands are at my throat and she slams me to the floor and presses into my neck, hard. I gasp for air, but nothing comes out. She continues to press even harder, my head thumping against the floor each time she pushes.

The room begins to spin. Lights, like little shooting stars, flash in front of my eyes as the room begins to fade to black. I'm losing consciousness. With the horrid, guttural sounds still coming from her throat, Carol repositions herself to straddle me, briefly loosening her grip. I manage to get a shallow breath before she tightens her grip around my neck. I try once more to take a breath, but the crush of her fingers on my throat prevents it.

Suddenly I hear a loud, blood-curdling scream followed by some shuffling, then Carol is no longer on top of me. I can't see anything, but I hear another voice. It's Tia's.

"What are you doing?!" Tia screeches.

Tia rushes to me. "Melon, oh, my God, I'm so sorry, I'm so sorry." I can see some movement next to my head and realize she's dialing her cell, crying aloud as she does.

"You're insane!" she screeches back at her mother. "And don't you dare move." I hear a thud and realize Carol has fallen to the floor. I think Tia may have pushed her.

I lie on the floor for what seems like hours, but, in reality, is probably only minutes. I can feel the cold night air blowing on me. Tia must have opened the back door. She squats next to me on the floor, sobbing. She leans over me and some of her tears fall onto my neck. The salt stings my skin where Carol's fingers had been moments earlier.

There's the sound of sirens, followed by a blur of chaos. Paramedics work quickly and methodically around me. A mask goes over my face and I hear brief discussions and medical terms, things I don't understand, things for which I'm relieved because it means I'm alive.

I'm on a gurney now, strapped down like a babe to her mother's back. I open my eyes. Cole's standing over me now, looking down. He doesn't speak. He takes my hand, his fingers cold but reassuring as he presses his palm into mine, telling me what I need to know: It's over.

EPILOGUE

Almost a month has passed since that twisted night at Think Ink, and it seems so crazy surreal now that it's as if it happened to another person, or was just some really bad movie I watched. But, of course, the reminders of its truth are here and ever present, and it will take time (forever, it seems) for things to become normal again.

I suffered a mild concussion and a badly bruised spine from the attack, and spent that night in the hospital for observation. I thought the doctors were going to have to hospitalize my parents that night, too, for they were (and still are, really) inconsolable after they learned that my father's own sister had tried to strangle their daughter, and that she, Carol, also murdered another person, and then hid the body years earlier.

My aunt confessed immediately to Barry's murder and cooperated fully with the police following her arrest. She is being held in the local county jail. I don't think either Tia or Bass has been there to see her.

Miriam Stevens, the local detective assigned to my aunt's case, has been to our home a couple of times now, keeping me and my parents apprised of anything new, including my aunt's arraignment. I was hoping it would be Cole's dad who knocked on our door, but he's in another division. It's from Miriam Stevens that we learned the circumstances of Barry Willet's death.

According to Carol's confession, Barry was, as others said, a very kind man who, for reasons I cannot begin to imagine, fell romantically for my aunt. He also cared very much for my cousins Bass and Tia, and, as Tia had told me, Barry had hoped to become a permanent part of the kids' and Carol's lives. But he soon learned Carol not only drank too much, but was taking prescription drugs, all while caring for her children.

It was on that doomed night at the campground that Barry confronted Carol and told her he was reporting her to Child Services for her drug and alcohol abuse. Carol, terrified of losing her children, killed Barry in a drunken rage, exactly as I saw it in my dreams. She dragged his body to a dense area and carefully concealed it under dirt in a remote cave among the caverns and crevices imbedded in the grassy hills of Blackfoot Springs. She went back once briefly, she said, to look for the single Nike shoe that had fallen off Barry's foot in the encounter.

The remains of Barry Willet have not yet been found, but the sheriff of Mahoning County says he's confident they'll find them. An early December snow has slowed the search.

I will go back to school after the holidays. It's been difficult being home all these weeks, mainly dealing with the fallout that my parents are experiencing, especially my mother. She is trying very hard to make up for not having believed me about any of it, and both of them for ever having left me in Carol's care. But the fact is they didn't believe me and they did leave me with Carol, and the sting of that betrayal will take time to go away. All three of us go to the therapist now. Twice we went together and twice I've gone alone. Who could have imagined any of that happening? Not me. Still, although it has been hard, I love my parents, and I know they love me, and I trust one day things will turn for the better when the time is right. It seems a long road ahead.

Hannah texted me when the news got out, which took about a nanosecond. I didn't read it until several days later.

> omg is it true? how's ur neck?
> how brave u r. V and I are here
> 4 u always.

I don't know if the news that I almost died at the hands of my aunt was so shocking that Hannah is making a genuine offer of peace, or if this is simply the biggest scoop she'll ever cover and needs to get close to the source. I think I know which it is.

Grandma Wren hasn't returned. I'm sure, like me, she didn't see that night at Tia's shop coming. I love my grandmother, but, just as with my parents—more so, really—I need time to forgive her because, as much as any player in that unfortunate night years ago, she is responsible for what I've endured. It was Grandma, like me, who accidentally witnessed Carol murder Barry. And it was she who told me I didn't see what I saw. She stole the truth from me to protect her own disturbed daughter. Once my grandmother saw what Carol had done, she had a choice to go to the police, but didn't. And being so young, I took the horror I witnessed and wove a story into my child mind, some of it exactly as it was, some of it not.

Cole's been over almost every day since I've been home from the hospital. Tyler's almost as happy about that as I am because Cole not only plays video games with him but has shown my brother how to improve his scores.

Sometimes Cole and I just sit on the sofa not saying anything. But it's a good silence, a silence that can be broken anytime either of us wants. It's just that sometimes we don't want to talk.

I know deep down in my soul that wherever our paths take us, Cole will, for the rest of my life, be a sacred part of me. It's Cole who never, not for one single moment, doubted my stories or my theories. True, he never believed I killed someone, but he did believe there was something to my dreams. He accepted what I said on faith and rode the crashing waves alongside me.

Tonight I lie in my bed wide awake. The old nightmares have stopped, but I sometimes fear what dreams lie ahead.

I look around my room and spot the book on my desk where I left it weeks earlier. I reach over and pick up the familiar play. I open to Act Three:

To sleep—perchance to dream: ay, there's the rub. For in that sleep of death what dreams may come.

I reread the tortured words of the troubled Hamlet and realize that my dreams—the ones to come—aren't those of which Hamlet speaks. I'm alive. I'm a real, living, breathing person, and so my dreams will be those of a living, breathing person who's very happy to be here.

Acknowledgements

Deepest love and gratitude to my daughters, Bridget and Gretchen, steadfast supporters from the very start; to Kirk, whose humor and insight inspire me; and to all my wonderful family and friends for their support.

A giant, colossal thanks to D.B. Gilles, my dear friend and mentor, without whom this book (or any of my plays) would not have been written. Merci beaucoup mon ami.

And to my awesome husband, Len, my love and my confidant, for the encouragement (and ear) throughout this very long process. Thank you, thank you!

About The Author

Margo Haas is a playwright, actor and novelist. Her published plays include adult, teen and young adult mysteries and comedies. She works in her native state of Ohio with kids from grade school through high school, teaching drama and playwriting workshops.

Contact Margo at
haasmargo@gmail.com

Made in the USA
Columbia, SC
19 October 2018